Natural DECEPTION

Other Books by Anna Durand

Natural Obsession (Au Naturel Nights, Book One)
Natural Passion (Au Naturel Trilogy, Book One)
Natural Impulse (Au Naturel Trilogy, Book Two)
Natural Satisfaction (Au Naturel Trilogy, Book Three)
Lachlan in a Kilt (The Ballachulish Trilogy, Book One)
Aidan in a Kilt (The Ballachulish Trilogy, Book Two)
Rory in a Kilt (The Ballachulish Trilogy, Book Three)
The American Wives Club (A Hot Brits/Hot Scots/Au Naturel Crossover Book)
Brit vs. Scot (A Hot Brits/Hot Scots/Au Naturel Crossover Book)
Dangerous in a Kilt (Hot Scots, Book One)
Wicked in a Kilt (Hot Scots, Book Two)
Scandalous in a Kilt (Hot Scots, Book Three)
The MacTaggart Brothers Trilogy (Hot Scots, Books 1-3)
Gift-Wrapped in a Kilt (Hot Scots, Book Four)
Notorious in a Kilt (Hot Scots, Book Five)
Insatiable in a Kilt (Hot Scots, Book Six)
Lethal in a Kilt (Hot Scots, Book Seven)
Irresistible in a Kilt (Hot Scots, Book Eight)
Devastating in a Kilt (Hot Scots, Book Nine)
Spellbound in a Kilt (Hot Scots, Book Ten)
Relentless in a Kilt (Hot Scots, Book Eleven)
Incendiary in a Kilt (Hot Scots, Book Twelve)
Wild in a Kilt (Hot Scots, Book Thirteen)
One Hot Chance (Hot Brits, Book One)
One Hot Roomie (Hot Brits, Book Two)
One Hot Crush (Hot Brits, Book Three)
The Dixon Brothers Trilogy (Hot Brits, Books 1-3)
One Hot Escape (Hot Brits, Book Four)
One Hot Rumor (Hot Brits, Book Five)
One Hot Christmas (Hot Brits, Book Six)
One Hot Scandal (Hot Brits, Book Seven)
One Hot Deal (Hot Brits, Book Eight)
Echo Power (Echo Power Trilogy, Book Two)
Echo Dominion (Echo Power Trilogy, Book Two)
Echo Unbound (Echo Power Trilogy, Book Three)
The Janusite Trilogy (Undercover Elementals, Books 1-3)
Obsidian Hunger (Undercover Elementals, Book Four)
Unbidden Hunger (Undercover Elementals, Book Five)
The Thirteenth Fae (Undercover Elementals, Book Six)
Cyneric (Undercover Elementals, Book Seven)

Natural DECEPTION

An Naturel Nights, Book Two

ANNA DURAND

JACOBSVILLE BOOKS · MARIETTA, OHIO

NATURAL DECEPTION

ISBN: 978-1-958144-26-8 (paperback)
ISBN: 978-1-958144-27-5 (ebook)
ISBN: 978-1-958144-28-2 (audiobook)

Manufactured in the United States.

Jacobsville Books
www.JacobsvilleBooks.com

Publisher's Cataloging-in-Publication Data
provided by Five Rainbows Cataloging Services

Names: Durand, Anna, author.
Title: Natural deception / Anna Durand.
Description: Marietta, OH : Jacobsville Books, 2023. | Series: Au naturel nights, bk. 2.
Identifiers: ISBN 978-1-958144-26-8 (paperback) | ISBN 978-1-958144-27-5 (ebook) | ISBN 978-1-958144-28-2 (audiobook)
Subjects: LCSH: Man-woman relationships--Fiction. | Vacations--Fiction. | Divorce--Fiction. | Middle-aged persons--Fiction. | Romance fiction. | BISAC: FICTION / Romance / Contemporary. | FICTION / Romance / Later in Life. | GSAFD: Love stories. | Humorous fiction.
Classification: LCC PS3604.U724 N38 2023 (print) | LCC PS3604.U724 (ebook) | DDC 813/.6--dc23.

Chapter One

Vanessa

A mature woman shouldn't do crazy things, which means the only conclusion I can reach about my mental health is that I've lost my mind. Why else would I accept an invitation to spend two weeks at a nudist resort in the South Pacific? A resort where clothing is forbidden and there are virtually no rules. I'm fifty-four years old, for heaven's sake. The most insane part of this whole adventure is that I jumped on a plane because I received a letter in the mail inviting me to do it.

You have won a free vacation at the Au Naturel Naturist Resort South Seas, the letter declared. *Leave your old life behind and embark on an adventure where nothing is forbidden. Live the fantasy for two weeks at this all-inclusive resort.*

"Ms. Stendahl, are you all right?"

I snap out of my trance and smile at the nice young man who stands behind the reception desk. "I'm fine, yes. My mind wandered for a minute, that's all.

"A lot of our guests experience the same thing when they land on Heirani Motu. They know it's a naturist resort, but they aren't fully prepared for what it's like." He offers me a cardboard folder and a keycard. "This is your welcome packet. We've set you up in a suite that overlooks the bay, and here's the key."

I've forgotten the sweet young man's name already, but fortunately, the employees here wear name tags. "Thank you, Emilio. You're the assistant manager, right?"

"Yes. James Bythesea, our general manager, will greet all the guests at the welcome ceremony. His wife, Holly, will be there too."

"When and where is the welcome ceremony?"

"In half an hour, on the main patio."

"Um, where is that?"

He grins and points behind me. "The main patio is right out there. You walked across it to get here."

"Right. Of course."

Yeah, I feel like a moron. Ever since my airline flight landed on Fiji at the Nausori International Airport, I'd gradually begun to feel like I'm entering an alternate universe. A small jet, piloted by an Australian who loves to gab, had brought me to this private island.

A bellhop leads me to my suite and carries all my bags inside while smiling and telling me how wonderful this island is. I'm getting the impression that the employees love this place as much as their guests must. I've been here for twenty minutes, and already I wish I could stay forever. I have a job and responsibilities waiting for me back home. My kids might be adults now, but I still feel like a mom who needs to take care of everyone.

Once I've tipped the bellhop, I finally take a moment to drink in the surroundings. What am I doing at a nudist resort? One where I am not allowed to wear clothes. If I want to visit Fiji or New Zealand while I'm here, I will need clothing. But on Heirani Motu, that's forbidden.

I glance down at my outfit. Should I strip now? Or wait until after the welcome ceremony? I grab the folder Emilio had given me and flip through the contents. On page one, it says, "Once you've checked in, please remove your clothing. This is a clothes-free resort." Okay, then. Time to strip.

Am I doing that yet? Not quite. I bite my lip. Then I kick off my sneakers and remove my gauzy overshirt, but I can't convince myself to take off the rest of my clothing.

Suck it up, woman. You're too old to give a damn what other people think of you.

I need to ease into this. That sounds like a good plan. So, I wander across the suite to the open patio. I can tell the glass doors as well as the windows that separate the patio from the suite itself are wide open, and there's a small hut out there too, which seems to be made of bamboo or palm fronds. I'm a high school science teacher, not a botanist.

But I need to forget about all that. For the next two weeks, I'm a nudist looking for a good time.

Oh, jeez. I sound like a teenage nymphomaniac.

I amble out onto the patio and admire the incredible scenery. The island of Heirani Motu boasts a big, jagged mountain and crystal-clear water surrounding it on all sides. But the most impressive element is, by far, the deep-blue sky. I live in America, where even tiny towns have skies marred by the contrails of airliners and other types of jets. But here, I can't see a single thing up there except for natural clouds. I wonder if this island is away from the commercial air traffic paths. Seems like it must be.

No more procrastinating. I strip off my clothes and toss them away, sucking in a deep, cleansing breath of tropical air.

But a breeze grabs my shirt, whisking it away.

"Shit!" I race to snatch it up before the shirt gets pulled away to who knows where, but the breeze picks up even more. "No, no, no!"

I slap my palms on the patio railing and curse under my breath. My shirt has flown away with the birds. Well, I am on a clothes-free island. Time to embrace the naughtiness.

Guests are starting to head for the main patio, though they don't seem to be in any hurry. We must have fifteen to twenty minutes left before we need to arrive at the patio for the welcome ceremony. I notice three men have stopped directly below my private patio. All of them are naked, of course. I can see the faces of two of them but the third man, who stands closest, has his back to me. His body captures my attention, and I can't stop admiring that physique. That's one tight ass. He must work out religiously. He has strong thigh muscles too, and his biceps could make even a ninety-year-old woman salivate.

Am I here for a fling? Or just to escape from my boring life back home? I'll think about the answer to that question later.

The hot guy saunters off with his friends and moves out of my sight.

Sighing, I walk back into the bedroom and dig my sandals out of my bags. This is the only clothing I'll need. I brush my hair and check my makeup, then hunt around in my purse to find the new shade I'd bought just before coming here. It's a brighter pink than I usually wear, but I decide to go for it. The last thing I do is glance down at my body to make sure I don't have any dirt on me.

No dirt. But I can see the faint scars from my hysterectomy. That's not sexy. All the workouts on earth won't get rid of that. So, I root around in my purse until I find the little bottle of foundation I'd stuffed in there. A quick patch job covers the scars well enough.

Now it's time to go.

I grab the wide-brimmed straw hat I'd bought at the Suva airport and stroll out to the main patio. A lot of people are here already.

And I see that hot guy again, though only from the back. I'd recognize that ass anywhere. My ex-husband had never cared about working out, and I didn't mind if he was slightly flabby. Well, not until he dumped me and started dating women who were inappropriately young for him.

I should not be thinking about Craig right now. This is my getaway, an adventure to spice up my life. My ex is probably knee deep in computer stuff right now, crammed into a cubicle in an office building, while I'm here on a gorgeous island surrounded by gorgeous men. I can take my pick.

A dark-haired woman steps out onto the patio and whistles loudly. "Listen up, folks! It's time for the welcome ceremony. Please pay attention because we will be giving you important information. I'm Holly Bythesea, guest services manager here at the Au Naturel Naturist Resort South Seas. If you need anything, feel free to ask me." Holly steps aside and spreads an arm. "And now, may I introduce the general manager, and my hubby, James Bythesea."

A dark-haired man walks out of the lobby and clasps Holly's hand. He waves to the guests. "Welcome to paradise. The island of Heirani Motu is privately owned and offers many opportunities to explore the landscape, on prepared trails or in the wild. But before you explore, we need to explain the rules." He smiles and winks. "There aren't many restrictions, so don't complain just yet."

Wow, that is one good-looking general manager. Do they only hire attractive people to work here? James Bythesea looks older, though not as old as I am. His wife seems much younger.

My gaze wanders over the crowd until I spot a familiar backside. Once the welcome speeches are over, I might go over there and introduce myself to the mystery man with the tight tush and thick biceps.

James continues his speech. "Remember, this is an adults-only, clothes-free naturist resort. The few exceptions to that rule are outlined in your packets. In consideration of our clothes-free mandate, we provide a few amenities other resorts don't. The terracotta bowls located throughout the resort proper offer free access to sunscreen, insect repellent, and condom packets. Our in-house pharmacy can also provide whatever medication refills you might need."

Condoms? My head swivels toward the man in charge. Is this a sex club? Not sure if I'm progressive enough to sign on for that. But the packet I was given said nothing about BDSM, so I assume the condoms are strictly there to ensure everyone practices safe sex.

I can't focus on whatever James Bythesea is saying now. Why? Because I can't stop staring at the mystery man. I'm too damn old to get infatuated with anyone, no matter how sexy he is. But simply watching his backside makes me feel warmer and wetter in ways that are not appropriate in public.

No doubt about it. I've been celibate for too long.

James has finished his speech, and the guests begin to spread out and head for their rooms or down the nature trails. The mystery man's friends have walked away, leaving him alone on the patio. Alone except for me. But he hasn't looked this way. I glance down at my breasts that aren't as perky as they once were and suffer a brief moment of panic. Then I suck it up and act like a mature woman, waltzing straight up to him. He's still facing away from me, so I tap his shoulder.

He turns around.

And I gape at him as cold rushes through my and throat tightens. "Craig? What the hell are you doing here?"

Chapter Two

Craig

My ex-wife is gaping at me like I have a nuclear weapon strapped to my chest and the countdown timer has five seconds to go. Is it so much of a shock that I might visit a nudist resort? Yeah, it is. But her shock still seems like overkill. I'm having trouble concentrating on what she said, though, because her nude body is distracting me. I've seen Vanessa naked more often than I could count. We were married for a long time, after all. But I swear she's more toned now than the last time I saw her.

That was two years ago. She looks better than ever.

I can't remember what she said, so I force myself to look her in the eye instead of in the tits. "Did you ask me a question?"

"Yes. What the hell are you doing here?"

"Taking some time off. You always said I was a workaholic, so you should be applauding me for kicking back for a change."

"But this is a nudist resort."

"I know that. Did you think I accidentally stumbled onto this remote island and decided to stay for a while?"

She plants her hands on her hips. "Why are you here, Craig? Nudism isn't in your comfort zone."

"Maybe I've expanded my zone." My gaze flicks down to her groin, and I cough into my fist as I zero in on her eyes again. "What are *you* doing here, anyway?"

Vanessa rubs her arms, a gesture I know well. It means she's uncomfortable and wishes aliens would land to whisk her away to

Jupiter so she wouldn't need to answer my question. Finally, she sighs. Her shoulders flag. "I got an invitation in the mail. It said I won a free two-week stay at the Au Naturel Naturist Resort South Seas."

"Since when do you jump on a plane because of a letter? You didn't even know if the offer was legit."

"I checked it out, obviously. Wasn't hard to find the resort website. Then I called the airline and found out there was a reservation for me." She lifts her brows. "What about you? What drew you to this place? You know I don't believe in coincidence."

Neither do I. Vanessa is too smart to believe whatever bullshit I might invent to explain away the situation. But I can't tell her the truth. She'd whack me on the head with a terracotta condom bowl. Yeah, there's one right behind her. I doubt she noticed. My ex-wife is laser focused on me, and she wants an answer to her question. What kind of lie can I believably feed her?

There's no way on earth that I'll tell her the truth. Not yet. I need to ease Vanessa into it.

"I got a letter too," I say. "We both lucked out, huh? I guess whoever sent out the invites thought we were still married."

"But you live at a different address, and I have a different last name."

Damn. I've always loved that she's whip smart, but right now, I wish Vanessa would develop a sudden case of the dumdums. "Uh, there are probably mailing lists that haven't caught up with the fact we're divorced. The post office must know to forward those to you."

"Uh-*huh.* Do you think I'm a moron?" I open my mouth to respond, but she throws a hand up to silence me. "I don't care how it happened. We're both here, and I intend to have a good time."

I open my mouth again.

She holds up a hand again. "We will not be vacationing together. This might be a small island, but we will steer clear of each other. Got it? I'll enjoy my vacation, and you can enjoy yours."

What else can I say? "Yeah, sure. Separate vacations."

Vanessa turns and walks away.

I can't resist watching her sexy ass while she sashays down a trail that leads into the woods. She doesn't trust me. She thinks I'm hiding something from her. And she's annoyed that I'm here, horning in on her tropical holiday at a naughty resort. Well, she's not wrong about that. I do have an ulterior motive, but it's not what she thinks.

Four hot young women amble by, and they all smile at me. One even winks.

Even if I wanted to find a holiday lover, I couldn't do it. A fifty-five-year-old divorced guy has no business trying to seduce nubile twenty-somethings. But that's not the reason I won't dip my toes into those waters.

I want my ex-wife back. I'm still in love with Vanessa.

Christ, I wish I'd realized a lot sooner that I would never love anyone else and that we just needed to spice up our lives. The divorce had been a mistake. Now I have two weeks to convince Vanessa of that.

How did we wind up on this island together? I sent her that letter.

A trio of women who seem a little older, probably in their forties, walk past me. They smile and wave. The only reason women are eying me like I'm a sirloin steak with all the fixings is because I spent the past year working out like a maniac—all to impress Vanessa.

I consider wandering down the trail she had taken, but I don't want to become a stalker. So, I head out to the pool on the other side of the main building. The pool snakes around that side of the resort and includes little huts where swimmers can kick back before they dive in again. I'd met a few people here earlier, but I don't fit in with the younger generations. They want to drink appletinis and check their cell phones every five seconds.

What's wrong with a cold beer and conversation?

I wind up bypassing the pool and going to my room instead. I came here to win back my wife. Can't do that by ordering room service and watching dirty pay-per-view movies. I want to fuck my ex-wife, not watch other people getting it on.

After twenty minutes of twiddling my thumbs, literally, I suck it up and head out to enact my evil plan. I need to convince Vanessa that we should never have split up and that I can give her the excitement she always wanted in the bedroom. I'd balked at playing games. It seemed... I don't know. Unmanly, I guess. If I'm ever going to seduce Vanessa into taking me back, first I need to seduce her into fucking me. I'm a data scientist, not a lothario. But I'm also pigheaded, as Vanessa always used to tell me.

So yes, I will get her back. I just have to hope she never finds out that I tricked her into coming to this resort.

I head out beyond the main patio, down the same trail Vanessa had taken earlier. Two young guys nod to me and smile as they pass by me, walking in the opposite direction. Everybody here seems happy, from the guests to the employees. I've felt more relaxed ever since the moment I stepped off that spiffy little plane and onto the solid ground of Heirani Motu. That's the only reason I have the balls to enact my plan.

Offshoot trails lead to various other locations on the island, and signs tell me where each one goes. I bypass the waterfall trail. Vanessa would be more likely to head for the beach on her first day here. Some of the young women who had admired me earlier walk past me now on their way back to the resort building. They smile and wink again. Jeez, don't these women have anything to do besides flirting with men? When I'd been a young guy, girls weren't so brazen.

Times change. But I'd rather rewind than fast forward.

At last, I reach the end of the trail and see the beach ahead of me. I hope it's not packed with young people. Or packed at all. I need to get Vanessa alone. Fortunately, it seems like not many guests have made it to the beach yet. I step onto the sand, swiveling my head left and right. I'm searching for ex-wife, of course. But I don't see her. Maybe she went somewhere else, like the waterfall. I could waste hours trying to find her. I didn't bring my phone with me because this is supposed to be an escape from reality, and a cell phone doesn't mesh with that idea. If I want to call Vanessa, I'll have to go back to my room to grab my phone.

Laughter erupts from further down the beach, beyond my sight.

I know that laugh. It's Vanessa. I jog down the beach and duck around an rock outcropping into a sheltered spot shaded by the fronds of a palm tree.

Vanessa sits on a towel with a muscular young man.

Oh, shit. Is she flirting with this guy? Is he flirting with her? I can't tell. They're both smiling, but I only heard Vanessa laughing. Her buff new friend can't be more than thirty, if that. He has a tattoo on his left arm, but the abstract pattern and colors don't scream "tough guy" to me. It seems more like he asked his little sister to choose a design for him.

I'm turning into such a fossil. Pretty soon, somebody will screw a name plate onto my chest that declares I'm the oldest example of the now-extinct computer geek species ever dug up from a tar pit.

Vanessa notices me, and her eyes go wide. "Craig?"

"Glad you remember my name. I am your husband, after all."

The buff young guy scrambles to move further away from Vanessa. "Oh, hey, sorry. I didn't know—"

"He is not my husband." She scowls at me. "We're divorced."

"Yeah, still don't think I want to get in the middle of this." The young guy gets up and gives her a tight smile. "See you around."

I cross my arms. "But we haven't even been introduced yet. I'm Craig Hathaway."

"Uh..." He eyes me like I might go thermonuclear any second, but then relaxes. "Nice to meet you, Craig. I'm Zach Moore. We can all be friends, right?"

"Yeah, sure." My tone probably didn't convince him.

"Well, I'll see you around."

Zach hustles away.

Vanessa jumps up and scowls at me again. "Whatever kind of game you're playing, I want no part of it. Go home."

"I paid for two weeks on this island."

"Just so you could harass me."

"You know I'm not like that. But since we're both here, why don't we talk about...things."

She sets her hands on her hips and gives me a suspicious look that I know well. "You are up to something, Craig. I don't like it. You never used to be so cagey, and you weren't the type to do anything sneaky. But I'm getting that vibe from you now."

How can I respond to that? She's right, of course. I am being cagey and sneaky, though for a good cause—in my opinion. She probably won't agree. That means I need to ease her into the idea that we belong together. The divorce was a mistake.

"We're not kids fresh out of college," Vanessa says. "We are adults heading toward retirement age. Please don't patronize me. Just be honest and tell me what is going on. Did you know I'd be here on this island? Did you have something to do with that?"

No, I can't answer that question. But I don't like lying to her, which leaves me with only one option—to sort of tell the truth. "Since we're both here, why don't we spend some time together and see what happens? We've been out of each other's orbits for too long, and it might be nice to just be friends."

She taps her fingers on her hips. Then she relaxes. "All right. Let's have a friendly chat."

"Great. We can go to the dining hall—"

"No. Let's talk at the waterfall. I saw it on the map of the resort, and it looks like it's a private place to hang out."

"Sure. Let's go there."

Chapter Three

Vanessa

We walk side by side while wending our way down the trails until we find the waterfall. It turns out to be a small clearing just big enough to hold two chaises. The fronds of a palm tree shade most of the space, but I also see other types of trees as well as flowering plants. This island really is beautiful and a true paradise on earth, the perfect place for weathering a midlife crisis.

I can't believe I just thought those words. *Midlife crisis.* It sounds so...trite and pathetic. I have a career I love and a family I love. What have I got to feel bad about?

Craig stretches out on one of the chaises.

I mull my options and decide to sit on the edge of the other chaise, facing him. "You keep saying you want to talk, so let's get it over with."

"You make a 'friendly chat' sound like sheer agony. Don't you remember how we used to lie in bed after the kids went to sleep and talk about anything and everything? I miss those chats."

"I'm not getting in bed with you."

He sighs and waves toward my chaise. "Why don't you at least lie down? This isn't supposed to be a torture session."

But it kind of feels that way. I used to love him and love our bedtime chats, but something changed after the kids all left home. We won't ever get back together as a couple, but maybe I should explain for both our sakes. "Look, I know we haven't seen much of each other over the past few years. But I would like us to be friends again, like we were before we started dating and got married."

"I'd like that too. But you were the one who moved out of our house because you needed 'space.' I forgave you for that."

"Yeah, I know. And I'm glad you believe we can be friends." I relax a little, but I still don't feel comfortable stretching out on my chaise. "What happened to us?"

He shrugs. "We stopped talking, and then our marriage gradually crumbled. I know I didn't try hard enough to fix things, and I regret that."

"Me too. Once the kids were out of the house, it seemed like we forgot how to communicate."

"Let's not turn this into a pseudo-therapy session."

I fold my arms over my chest. "Why wouldn't you go to couples therapy with me? I was trying to work things out."

"Yeah, that's the problem. *You* were trying to work things out."

"What is that supposed to mean?"

"That you didn't really want couples therapy. You wanted an hour of bashing me so you could feel better about yourself."

Oh, God, we're falling into the same trap all over again. Bickering doesn't help anything. "Therapy didn't work for us. I know we both agree on that. But something deeper was coming between us, and I felt like you didn't care about figuring out what the problem was or trying to fix it."

"That's bullshit. I tried to make you happy, but you wouldn't let me in. How can I help if we don't talk to each other?"

My attempt to move past the bickering has blown up in my face. I don't blame Craig for that. We both made bad decisions. "I want us to be friends. That means we don't need to argue about who's to blame for this or that. We just need to be cordial with each other. Can you manage that?"

He rolls his eyes. "Of course I can."

I really don't miss the eye-rolling. Craig is the only person I've ever met who does that.

"What now?" he asks. "We made our peace agreement."

"And that means we're done." I get up and give him a polite smile. "See you around the island. I hope you have a wonderful vacation."

I turn to walk away.

"Where are you going? We aren't done talking."

"Yes, we are." I glance over my shoulder at him. "We agreed to be casual friends, and there's nothing left to say."

"That's crap." He jumps off his chaise. "We're supposed to hash out our differences."

"When did we agree to that?"

He spreads his arms wide. "The whole time we've been talking. What did you think I wanted? To give you a friendship bracelet? I want to get back together."

My eyes have begun to burn, and I think that's because they're bulging. Craig has lost his mind. I experience a bizarre impulse to hit him with a palm frond repeatedly, but I'm too old to behave that way. So instead, I roll my shoulders back and clear my throat. "We are never reconciling, Craig. I'm sorry. I will always care about you, but not in a romantic way. It's time we both moved on—for good."

This time, I do walk away and don't look back.

As I make my way back to the resort proper, I keep getting flashbacks of our marriage. But I don't recall the arguments. No, my mind insists on tormenting me with memories of all the good times—the backyard barbecues, the kids' birthdays, Christmas mornings, the way Craig used to brush hair away from my cheek, the way we made love like it was the first time every time. The sex wasn't wild or even particularly imaginative. But it felt like we were in sync, creating a sensual rhythm all our own.

I stop dead in the middle of the trail. I can see the resort building up ahead, but I can't convince my feet to move even one step further. No, I am not still in love with Craig. That would be insane. We broke up for a damn good reason, and I won't skip down memory lane with him like nothing happened.

What was the damn good reason? I can't remember anymore.

Of course I do. Don't I? The sex had gotten stale, but that wasn't the reason. The kids had all moved out and started their own lives, but that's not the reason either.

"Hey, Vanessa, there you are."

I whirl around and find my beach buddy striding up the path toward me. I can't help grinning at him. "Hi, Zach, it's great to see you again."

The hot young man trots up to me and smiles. "I was hoping I'd see you again. Didn't want to get in between you and your ex, but if you're free now..."

"Yes, I am totally free." I can't believe I just used the word *totally* in that context. I sounded like a horny teenager. Oh, who cares. I'm on a naughty nudist island, for pity's sake. "Zach, would you like to have lunch with me?"

"In the dining hall? Or someplace else?"

"Anywhere that's private."

"I'd love to have lunch with you, Vanessa. You're the hottest woman I've ever met."

Has anyone ever called me that before? Craig used to tell me I was beautiful, but he never called me the hottest woman he'd ever seen. I'm here to have a good time, so I might as well embrace the age-gap insanity. Maybe I'm having a midlife crisis, but I don't give a damn.

I offer my hand to Zach. "Let's go to the dining hall just to grab some food, then enjoy our lunch at the waterfall."

"Sounds awesome." He clasps my hand. "I'm so glad I bumped into you again."

"And so am I."

While we walk, we talk and laugh about how strange it is to be naked all the time, what we hope to do during our stay here, and how beautiful the island is. That means our journey takes at least twice as long as it would otherwise. Who cares? I've never been courted by a twenty-something man, and I can't deny I'm enjoying the attention. Do I want to date him? Probably not. I wouldn't mind a vacation fling, though.

No, I can't do that. It's something young people do, not post-menopausal women.

On our way out of the dining hall, we bump into Craig. *Perfect.* I was hoping to steer clear of him for a while, and maybe I would rather not have him see me with my very young companion. But I have nothing to be ashamed of, right? I'm an adult with no entanglements, not these days. I don't even have kids to take care of anymore.

Yet somehow I feel guilty now, all because we bumped into my ex-husband.

Craig glances at the picnic basket Zach is carrying. "You had a picnic in the dining hall? I didn't see that on the itinerary."

Zach laughs. "No, we didn't do that. We got some food, and now we're heading out to have a picnic. Didn't you read about that in the welcome packet? The resort provides baskets."

"Sorry, I didn't memorize the whole welcome packet."

Craig sounds a bit peevish now, but Zach hadn't said anything nasty. He was politely pointing out the facts. My ex has no business getting jealous.

I ignore Craig and curl my arm around Zach's. "Let's go. I'm starving."

Zach seems a touch confused, like he expects me to explain why I'm having a picnic with him, but honestly, I have no obligation to do that. I just want to have a nice, relaxing lunch with a friend who happens to be a man. A very young man.

"Nice to see you again," Zach tells Craig as we walk past him. "This place has awesome food. Can't wait to see what's on tap for dinner."

Thankfully, Zach starts walking away, so I don't need to say anything else to my ex-husband. He looks mildly annoyed, which I suppose is a step up from very insulted.

I wave to Holly Bythesea and the desk clerk as we exit the building. They both smile and offer us cheerful greetings. Then Zach takes me down the main trail until we reach the sign that points to the waterfall, and we veer down that path. I haven't seen much of the outdoors part of the resort, and I can't stop gawking at the scenery. Gorgeous tropical flowers. Towering green trees. I hear the songs of exotic birds and even glimpse a few of the brightly colored creatures, like parakeets, doves, hornbills, and minivets. I might have studied a South Pacific birdwatching book during the thirty-six-hour flight to Fiji. I won't tell Zach that. He might think I'm a geek, which I absolutely am. This is a teacher's paradise.

My first glimpse of the waterfall takes my breath away. It towers above us, the spray misting onto our bodies even from twenty feet away. The spray generates a faint rainbow too. This should be a romantic setting that makes me want to start something with the attractive younger man sitting beside me. But it doesn't. I probably just need time to adjust to my environment.

Zach brushes the backs of his fingers across my cheek. "You are so beautiful, Vanessa. Would you mind if I kissed you?"

"We haven't even had lunch yet."

He laughs affectionately. "Is that a rule now? Nobody told me. Food first, kissing after, huh?"

"It's not a rule. I'm famished, that's all." I must be rustier at dating than I realized. I hadn't needed to remember how to do this for a long, long time.

Zach and I cross the bridge to the other side of the ravine, where there's a nice little spot for picnicking. We engage in more mundane conversation that somehow manages to be fun too, while we enjoy the delicious meal the resort staff made for us.

We've just closed up our picnic basket when it starts to rain. I remember the welcome packet mentioned frequent afternoon showers that occasionally include some thunder. Zach takes my hand, guiding me toward the trunk of a palm tree where the long, wide fronds shelter us from the rain. The patter of the drops on the leaves makes me slightly aroused, and my nipples tighten. Zach takes that as an invitation, leaning in, aiming for my lips.

But he stops inches away from my mouth. "May I kiss you, Vanessa? It's all right if you don't want me to."

I appreciate his politeness, but I'm from a different generation. My first kiss with Craig hadn't involved a request. I looked at him just as he looked at me, and then our lips met. If hadn't wanted the kiss, I would have told him so. But Zach seems to think I need to be reminded that I can say no. It's kind of sweet, but also a stark reminder that we come from very different worlds.

Do I want to kiss him? What the hell. Might as well find out what it feels like to make out with a twenty-something. "I'd like it if you kissed me, Zach."

"Awesome." He leans in a little more. "Still time to change your mind."

Oh, for pity's sake. I said yes already, but he thinks I need more time to consider the horrific consequences of letting him kiss me. "Don't want to change my mind, promise."

Finally, he touches his lips to mine.

And I feel...nothing. He has soft lips, but I don't experience any kind of desire for him despite his hot body and sweet personality. I'm just not attracted to him.

I lay a hand on Zach's chest and gently push him away. "Sorry, sweetie, this isn't working for me."

"Yeah, I figured." He sighs. "Worth a shot, though, right?"

"Uh-huh." Movement beyond his shoulder spurs me to peer around his body, where someone has just stepped onto the bridge. "Oh, shit. My ex is here."

Chapter Four

Craig

My ex-wife's boy toy whirls around and smiles at me like we're best buds, and I brought a twelve-pack of beer. "Craig? Hey, bro, what's up? Me and Vanessa were having a picnic, but that rainstorm popped up and we had to find shelter. Isn't it weird that this island has rain almost every day?"

"It's the South Pacific," I point out. "What did you expect? A desert?"

"We already had dessert. If we'd known you were coming, we would've saved some for you."

This guy can't be as dumb as he sounds right now. He thinks "dessert" and "desert" are the same thing? Despite the fact he was kissing my ex-wife, I'll give him the benefit of the doubt and assume he's nervous because I caught him making out with Vanessa.

My underhanded grand plan hasn't worked out quite the way I'd hoped. Not yet.

Zach clears his throat and winces. "Uh, I think I should go find my friends. The picnic was fun, Vanessa. Hope I'll see you around the resort."

He hustles away, leaving me alone with Vanessa. I walk across the bridge to the spot where lover boy had kissed her. "Are you planning to screw that kid?"

"That is none of your business."

"At least give me the chance to prove middle-aged men can do it better."

She rolls her eyes. "No games, Craig. We're too old for that shit."

"Maybe we are." I move closer, forcing her to back up to the tree, and set my arm on the trunk beside her head. "Just let me kiss you once, to see if there's still any spark between us."

"Zach asks permission for everything."

"He's young and inexperienced. I'm not." I move even closer, penning her with both my arms now. "It's a yes or no question. Do you want me to kiss you?"

"You *are* doing exactly what Zach did—asking permission. Either do it or don't. Getting wishy-washy doesn't impress me."

"I'm not wishy-washy." I lean in, bending my arms until my chest meets her breasts. "I'm going to kiss you, Vanessa. Right now."

She stares into my eyes, tracing her tongue over her bottom lip.

Now or never. I cover her mouth with mine and hold that position for a moment, giving her time to react before I push for more. Her entire body relaxes, and her eyes flutter shut. *Bingo.* I press my mouth to hers more firmly as I slip my tongue between her lips and plaster my body to all her curves. Damn, she's even sexier than I remember, with toned muscles and a taut ass. I can't help sliding one hand behind her to cup one of those cheeks.

A soft moan sighs out of her.

I push my tongue deeper, rubbing my dick against her while it gradually firms up, readying for what we both want. She grips my biceps. I tease the roof of her mouth. She sinks her nails into my arms, and I don't care. It's been too damn long since I kissed Vanessa, even longer since I made love to her.

She wraps one leg around mine.

I pull my head back, breathing hard. "Let's have sex right here under this palm tree."

She just stares at me, seeming slightly dazed.

"Fuck, I want you so much." I wrap one arm around her to pull her away from the tree. "This is a nice soft spot for making love."

Vanessa freezes.

I open my mouth to ask what's wrong but don't get the chance.

She slaps me. "You bastard. The jerk who filed for divorce doesn't get to seduce me ever again."

My ex-wife marches across the bridge and down the trail.

And I stand here with half an erection and no chance of getting off, unless I want the DIY version. What just happened? She wanted me, I know she did. I said I wanted her and that this was a nice spot for making love. None of that should've set her off. She got so turned on that I could smell the scent of her cream wafting around us. Yet she called me a bastard and stormed off.

Okay, yeah, I did file for divorce. But she didn't fight it.

I'm too old to play the petty blame game. We broke up, and I still understand why, not really, not completely. It seemed like the right thing to do at the time. Now, I regret it. That's why I tricked her into coming to this resort, but I didn't really have a game plan for what I'd do once I got Vanessa here.

A data scientist ought to know how to do that. My job is to collate data and figure out how to organize it all while finding answers to questions brought up by the data itself. Yet I couldn't think far enough ahead to properly seduce my ex-wife. My dick took over. That's the problem. I need to summon my inner data scientist and study Vanessa.

Well, at least my erection has faded away. I can return to the resort without looking like a predator on the make.

Once I reach the main patio, I realize no one else is here. I sit down at a table that's shaded by an umbrella and mull my options. My ex-wife is not a dataset I can analyze and interpolate.

When a resort employee comes over to ask if I want anything to eat or drink, I sigh and slump back in my chair. "Got any booze?"

"Do you like rum?" she asks. "We have an excellent selection, and a lot of our guests love our mojito. It has rum, lime juice, mint, sugar, and sparkling water. Most people like that it has the vibe of a tropical drink."

"Yeah, sure, I'll have that." I'm more of a beer drinker, and I don't even drink that very often. But this is a tropical vacation. Might as well try the fruity beverages on hand. Just nothing with an umbrella. Fortunately, my cocktail does not come with one of those.

I'm halfway through my mojito when a shadow falls over me. A large one. I look and up try for a smile that doesn't quite get there. "Hey, James, what's up?"

The general manager sits down on the other side of the table. "I should ask you that question. You don't seem to be having a good time."

I shrug. "My plans haven't panned out so far."

"What plans are those?"

"Rather not say. It's embarrassing."

James chuckles. "I am the king of embarrassing debacles. Tell me what's on your mind, and perhaps I can help. Anything you say will be kept in strictest confidence."

"You don't need to play shrink for me. I'm a big boy, and I can work out my problems on my own."

"What I'm trying to say, in a round-the-houses sort of way, is that I believe I might have some personal insight to offer. My experiences with Holly, back when we first met, may be relevant."

I raise my brows. "Round the houses?"

He smiles. "It's a British term. It means I am, as you Americans might put it, beating round the bush."

"Maybe we should give the direct route a try."

"I agree." He leans back in his chair, folding his hands over his belly. "If I'm wrong about this, feel free to tell me to bugger off. But I suspect I'm right. You and I have a similar tendency to avoid direct confrontation. You want to reconcile with your ex-wife, yes?"

"You hit the nail on the head."

"Then would I also be correct in suggesting that you maneuvered Vanessa into coming to Heirani Motu?"

"Damn, you're good." I hook one ankle over the other knee and take a nice long swig of my mojito. The trendy drink is growing on me. "Maybe you should have been a psychologist instead of the general manager at a nudist resort."

"I'm happy where I am. But you're trying to evade my question."

"Guilty as charged." I set down my glass and wince. "I, uh, sent Vanessa a letter informing her that she'd won a free two-week stay at the Au Naturel Naturist Resort South Seas."

The general manager smirks. "What made you choose a naturist resort for your nefarious plot?"

I wince even harder and scratch my cheek. "Well, I got online and searched for unusual vacation options. Took me three weeks of hunting before I found this place. It sounded perfect."

"For what? Seducing your ex-wife, obviously. But I suspect there's more to it."

"Yeah." This might be the most humiliating conversation I've ever had with another man. But he seems to genuinely want to help, and I'm screwing everything up on my own. "I spent the last year getting in shape. I wasn't a flabby loser before that, but I wanted to get buff to, ah, impress Vanessa."

James chuckles. "I had a suspicion that was the case. But did Vanessa do the same thing? Does she seem fitter now?"

"Definitely. Not a lot buffer. She looked great to start with, but she seems to have worked out a little more since the last time I saw her."

"When was the last time?"

"Two years ago."

He studies me for a moment. "When was your divorce finalized?"

"Three years ago."

"And how soon did you realize you'd made a mistake?"

"Six months later."

James tips his head to the side, seeming to study me with even more interest. "Don't do what I did with Holly. I tricked her in a way not unlike what you've done. But you have the chance to nip the problem in the bud. I suggest you think about that. The longer you wait, the more upset Vanessa will be when she learns the truth."

"I know. But I was hoping I could just forget about the letter stunt and move on to genuinely trying to win her over."

James pushes his chair back and rises. "I need to get back to work. But trust me, Craig, the truth will always out."

He strides back into the lobby.

I know I should take his advice. I know it's the right thing to do. But I've waited a long time to get Vanessa alone and tell her how I feel. Nothing has gone the way I'd hoped. If I confess that I deceived her, she might never speak to me again. Being a coward won't solve the problem. I'm a middle-aged man who should know better than to do what I've done.

But I love my wife. I want her back. And I don't see any other way to convince her that we belong together.

The truth will always out. James made that his parting advice to me. I don't know the details of how James tricked Holly, but it definitely worked out in the end. They're married and running this resort together.

I can't tell Vanessa what I did. Not yet.

After finishing off my mojito, I go inside to check out the gift shop. What else have I got to do? I find the usual gift-shop fare, like postcards and novelty shirts, but then I come upon something that confuses me. It's a bin full of party masks. The kind you might wear at a masquerade ball. I've never been to any event like that, so maybe these masks have another purpose that I'm not aware of, being a stuffy old guy.

A pretty young woman comes up beside me and sorts through the masks a little too casually. She picks one up and bites her lip, then turns to me. "Do you think this looks good on me?"

"Sure. Doesn't everyone look good in black?"

"Don't know." She drops the mask into the bin and pulls out another one, holding it up to my face. The girl grins. "You'd look super hot in this one. It's like *Phantom of the Opera*."

"So, I'd look hot dressed up as a psycho who lives in an underground cesspit."

"What's a cesspit?"

"No place anyone would want to go. It's kind of like a sewer."

She wrinkles her nose. "Ew. But I still think you'd look hot in this mask."

I push her hand away gently. "Thanks for the advice, but I don't need a mask."

Fortunately, two of her friends show up and whisk her away. Maybe Vanessa likes getting cozy with twenty-somethings, but I have no interest in that. I can't date someone who's younger than my adult children. James Bythesea might have married a much younger woman, but he can get away with that because he's British. I might've just invented that loophole, but I do know women love men who have British accents. My daughters do, anyway.

What about Vanessa? Maybe I should practice cultivating a British accent and see if that impresses her. Ahhh, I can smell the fetid odor of midlife desperation.

The nice young woman who manages the gift shop wanders past me, but she stops and turns back toward me. Her name tag identifies her as Mariel. "Do you need any help, sir?"

Like a lot of the employees at this resort, she speaks with an Australian or New Zealand accent. I have trouble telling the difference. It's kind of like American versus Canadian.

I'm about to say no to her question, but then I think of something. "Actually, you could solve a mystery for me."

"What is it?"

I hold up another mask. "Why do you sell so many of these?"

"We hold the occasional masquerade party. And, well..." She glances around furtively, then edges closer to me and whispers, "Some people like using the masks for, um, private enjoyment."

I can't help chuckling. "I catch your drift. Thanks for clearing that up."

Yeah, it was hard to misunderstand her drift after the way she looked around like she's an escaped felon. Some of the guests like to play sex games with masks. I wonder if Vanessa might like that.

Maybe it's time I found out.

Chapter Five

Vanessa

I spent most of the afternoon just trying to avoid my ex-husband. Craig kissed me. I should have told him not to do that, but instead, I closed my eyes and reveled in the kiss. It had been too long since the last time he pressed his mouth to mine and made me feel so warm and liquid, like I might fall into a puddle at his feet. Even before the divorce, we'd lost that spark—sexually and emotionally.

Maybe I felt a twinge of the old spark this afternoon. But we can't get back together. It's too late, and we're too old.

Craig doesn't look like a middle-aged father of three grown children. No, he could compete with the hottest young men on this island. More than compete. He blows them away with his mature sex appeal and impressive muscles.

I didn't know a man could look that good after fifty unless he's a movie star with a great plastic surgeon. Craig hasn't had cosmetic surgery. He definitely started working out more, though.

To distract myself from the Craig issue, I head over to the far side of the resort building where guests are playing a very strange game. It's called miniten, which I know because I read every word in my welcome packet. Miniten was invented by nudists way back when, and it's designed to be low impact. Nudists don't want their bits flapping.

I watch two pairs of guests hitting a tennis ball with a wedge-shaped wooden box that's apparently called a thug. The player shoves their hand into the thug, which has a handle bar inside it for the player to grip. If I'd thought pickle ball was weird—which I do—miniten blows that sport out of the park. By the time I've watched an entire game, I've decided I might want to participate in a match sometime during my stay. Not today, though. I've barely gotten settled in.

What time is it now? I have my phone in a little case that has a long strap, and I'd slung it over my shoulder. Now, I pull the phone out to check the time. It's five thirty. It's probably jet lag, but I'm already hungry. I can't eat now. That would put me in early-bird special territory, and I'm not that old yet.

I wander into the main building and head down to the game room, strictly to waste some time. Younger people are enjoying pinball, video games, foosball, air hockey, and mini bowling. This is an adults-only resort, but they offer kiddie games. I guess they just want everyone to have fun in any way they like.

A man throws up his hands as a pinball machine makes all sorts of noises that indicate the player won. He spins around, arms raised, and whoops.

That's Zach.

When he notices me, his grin morphs from joyful to...something else. He talks to his buddies briefly, then starts walking toward me.

I experience a powerful urge to turn and run away, but that would be childish. Instead, I wait and smile patiently as he approaches me. "Congratulations on winning the pinball game, Zach."

"Thanks." He leans toward me just a little and lowers his voice to a husky whisper. "I found a book in the gift shop that's all about sexy games adults can play in private."

Oh, shit. He still thinks I want him to seduce me. I should've been firmer about rebuffing his advances after that kiss earlier. Time to break his little heart. Well, it's more like shattering his horny plans. "That's nice, Zach, but I'm not interested. You are a sweet kid, and I'd love for us to be friends, but that's all. I'm not attracted to you."

He sighs, and his shoulders sag. "Yeah, I figured. Had to give it one last try, though. I hope I didn't offend you."

"Don't worry about it." I pat his arm. "There are lots of single women here. You won't have any trouble getting dates."

"If you change your mind, I'm ready and waiting."

Zach wanders away.

Never in my life have I been pursued by a younger man, or by a man my own age—with one exception. Craig had pursued me in the sweetest, most charming way when we met back in our college days. I fell for him so fast and so hard that I was sure we'd spend the rest of our lives together like a fairy-tale couple. It must've been true love, that's what I believed back then. But since then, I've learned fairy tales are for children and soul mates are a myth.

I wouldn't be divorced if such things did exist.

The game room doesn't seem enticing, so I start to head for the dining hall. But I halt at the door. My tummy grumbles, telling me I should ignore my silly hang-up about early-bird specials. This is an adults-only naturist resort. People who want to be buck naked for two whole weeks won't care when I choose to have dinner. Now that I've shaken off my phobia, I waltz into the dining hall.

Only a few people are here. Mostly couples. Not seniors, but definitely not the Gen Z set either. I'll be eating alone while everybody else has a special someone with them.

"You got hungry early too, huh?"

My stomach crashes to the floor, figuratively speaking, because that's my ex-husband's voice I hear behind me. I shuffle around to face him. "Hi, Craig. Did your date abandon you?"

"Date? I don't have one of those."

"But I saw you flirting with a hot young woman in the gift shop. She seems very into you."

He grins. "Are you jealous? That's cute. I talked to a girl, but I was only being polite. You must have been stalking me to know where I've been. But you spent the day with a hot young man, so we're even. At least I didn't kiss that girl."

"I wish I hadn't kissed Zach. He's a sweet kid, but I'm not interested in a May-December romance."

Craig stares at me. "You aren't hooking up with him?"

"No, of course not." I lift my brows. "Since when do you say 'hooking up'? We're both too old to adopt slang our kids might use."

He grimaces. "Yeah, we are."

I turn halfway toward the tables, eying those couples. Though I don't want to give him false hope that we'll get back together, I don't want to eat alone either. So, I concede this one battle. "Would you like to share a table with me? We both might feel less pathetic if we don't eat alone."

"Sure, let's do that. We might be the oldest people at this resort."

"Oh, no. I saw a couple who must be in their sixties, maybe even their seventies."

He wipes a hand across his forehead. "Whew. I don't need to ask for the senior discount after all."

"No one would mistake you for a senior citizen."

We don't need to worry about losing our table since hardly anyone is here yet, so we go straight to the buffet and load up our plates. Then we sit down and dig in. The silence is rather awkward, but I'm too hungry to care. By the time we finish eating, more people have started to arrive, though most of them grab snacks rather than meals. Craig and I walk out of the dining hall together, but we stop a little ways down the corridor.

I can tell he's anxious about something. "Spit it out, Craig. I know what it means when you scratch your elbow and your nose. Just tell me whatever it is."

"What? I had no idea I had a tell."

"You do. So, what's up?"

He scratches his elbow and nose again. "I was wondering if you'd like to go for a walk with me. I hear there's a trail that leads up the mountain. The welcome brochure said it's a great spot for watching the wildlife."

"That sounds nice. But to be honest, I'm jet-lagged. Think I'll just go to bed."

"Maybe another time?"

I hesitate but then opt for truthfulness. "Yeah, maybe another time."

No, I don't want to have sex with him. But exploring the island with a buddy is appealing. Why can't a divorced couple be friends?

The next morning, I wake up early since I'd gone to sleep early too. I blame jet lag. But now, I should be pretty much adjusted to the new schedule. I've just gotten out of the shower when someone knocks on the door to my suite. I'm in the middle of blow-drying my hair, so I holler "just a minute" while I struggle to unplug the hair dryer without electrocuting myself. Then I rush to the door and yank it open.

Craig eyes me up and down, his brows hiking up. "Did you stick your finger in the electrical socket?"

"What? No, of course not."

"Just wondered. I've only ever seen your hair this disheveled after we had sex." He smirks. "Or that time when a spider fell into your hair and you were scrambling to get rid of it while shrieking."

"I was not shrieking."

He leans against the jamb. "Wanna have breakfast together?"

"Okay. But this is not a date."

"Whatever you say. Got any plans for later?"

"No."

He folds his arms over his chest. "Well then, let's hike up that wildlife trail."

"As friends. No hanky-panky."

Craig laughs. "Hanky-panky? Can't remember ever hearing you say that before."

I don't think I ever have used that phrase before. But seeing him first thing in the morning has knocked me off kilter. Can't explain why. "We can do the nature hike, but I need food first."

"Me too." He points one finger at my head. "Might want to brush your hair first. Somebody might think we screwed each other's brains out before breakfast."

A silky warmth shimmers through me, though I did not want to feel this way. He made an offhand comment. I shouldn't get turned on by that. I shake off the feeling and sprint back into the bathroom to brush my hair. When I come back, Craig is still standing there leaning against the jamb.

I can't deny that my ex-husband is sexy. He always was, even before he decided to work out more and build up his muscles. I've always loved his body, but that mattered less to me than the way he made me feel when we were making love.

We head for the dining hall side by side, but not hand in hand. Not sure why I felt the need to mention that in my own thoughts. Do I need to convince myself of something? No, that's crazy. We're too old to get fluttery tummies and give each other shy smiles.

A hot young woman sashays past us just as we're entering the dining hall, but Craig only gives her a polite smile. He barely even looked at her. That girl had perfect tits and a perfect figure, the kind of body that every straight man on earth would want to admire. Since he obviously came to this island for the naughty atmosphere, I can't understand why he hasn't done anything, well, naughty.

The breakfast crowd has already filled the hall, so Craig wends through the crowd hunting for an open table, keeping in step with me all the while rather than rushing ahead. He grabs a small table that's just big enough for the two of us, then pulls a chair out for me. I sit down, at his polite insistence.

"You save our table," he says. "I'll get the food. Pretty sure I still remember what you like."

"Okay. Thanks."

I watch him walking toward the buffet, but I'm not admiring his ass this time. I stare at his backside in sheer disbelief. He's being courteous and sweet. Our marriage had gradually dwindled after our kids left home, and we sort of gave up on conversation and courtesy. Why has he suddenly changed his attitude? I can't tear my gaze away from him as he snatches up two plates and loads them up with breakfast foods. Then he hurries back to me to set down the plates. He flashes me a quick smile before he trots over to the beverage section and returns a moment later with drinks for us.

Craig finally sits down opposite me. "Go on and eat. Don't know about you, but I'm starving. Must be the jet lag."

"Yeah, I'm hungry too."

But instead of eating, I stare at him while he starts munching on papaya slices in between gnawing on a big, thick sausage. Every time he hacks off another piece of that meat, he opens his mouth wide and slips the sausage in there, sealing his lips while he slowly pulls the tines free. And he moans like a man who just had the best sex ever. Never in my life have I equated sex with sausage, but I suddenly can't shake that metaphor out of my mind. When Craig spears a piece of papaya and pushes the fork into his mouth, he wraps his lips around it and moans again. As he pulls the tines free, a bit of juice dribbles down his chin.

And I experience the most bizarre urge to lean across the table and lick it off.

"You okay, Nessa?"

My focus abruptly veers away from his mouth and up to his eyes. I clear my throat and scoop up a spoonful of my fruit salad. "Yeah, fine, great."

Did he just call me Nessa? He hasn't used that nickname in years. That's why I'm feeling...off balance. It's not because I want him to lay me across the table and fuck me right here in the dining hall. Mature adults don't do things like that.

I shove the yogurt-drenched fruit into my mouth and chew a little too vigorously. A slice of banana drops out of my mouth and onto my left breast.

Craig leans over to pluck it off my skin, then uses his napkin to wipe away the yogurt. "All better. Have some coffee to wake yourself up. You must still be kind of sleepy, hey?"

No, I'm not. I am wide awake, mentally—and thoroughly awakened in other ways that I prefer not to examine. But I tell him, "Yeah, I guess I'm not fully recovered from the jet lag yet."

I grab the cup of coffee he'd brought me and force myself to sip it instead of guzzling the drink. My brows shoot up. "You remember how I like my coffee?"

"With cream and two sugars, plus a shot of peppermint. I was surprised the resort had so many options for coffee."

"Yeah, me too."

Craig, of course, prefers his coffee black, no sugar, no nothing to spice it up. He also brought me a glass of orange juice.

Well, that's what I assume it is until I take a sip. "Is this a mimosa?"

"Yep. I remember how much you liked the mimosas we had at your aunt's birthday party a few years ago."

"Angela wanted a tropical-themed party, and she does love a good cocktail."

But he remembered I liked them, when I'd only ever had that drink once, and it was years ago. Craig never let on that he'd memorized my food and beverage preferences. Yes, I love Greek yogurt fruit salad too, as well as whole wheat pancakes with wheat germ and maple syrup. Did he bring me those items too? Yes, he did. My plate is chock-full of my favorites.

I might need to rethink my opinion of my ex-husband.

Chapter Six

Craig

Vanessa seems confused, or maybe dazed is a better word for it. She can't be shocked that I know all her favorite foods and drinks. We were married for more than three decades, after all. Doesn't she know all my likes and dislikes? She might have banished that information from her mind after the divorce, I suppose. But I remember everything about her. I should never have walked away from our marriage, and I will make things right with her no matter what it takes.

Yeah, like tricking her into coming to Heirani Motu.

Vanessa never needs to know about that. But once we've reconciled, maybe I should confess. I'll worry about that later.

I probably shouldn't have wiped yogurt off her breast. But it was an unconscious reaction. That means I need to apologize. "Sorry, Ness—Vanessa. I shouldn't have touched you that way, but it wasn't on purpose."

She gives me a tight smile. "I know that. Let's just forget it happened."

And that's what we do for the rest of breakfast. I try to engage her in conversation, but that one stupid, unconscious mistake has clearly upset her more than she wants to admit. I feel like smacking myself in the forehead, but I decide to do that in my mind rather than actually smacking myself. Vanessa would think I've gone completely insane if she saw me doing that.

Why do I keep feeling like a teenage geek who can't get the girl? Wooing has never been my strong suit, but somehow I'd managed to convince Vanessa to fall for me and marry me. I'm too old for that shit now. So, I'll need to come up with another way to get back into her good graces.

The only plan I've come up with so far is to seduce her. Hot sex will fix our relationship, right? I suppress a groan. The data scientist in me knows how to collate information and come up with a strategy to improve whatever situation might arise. But none of that helps me with the problem of Vanessa.

Sex it is, then.

That's not a plan, though. Now that I've got her on this island, away from all our family and friends, I have no fucking idea what to do next. I could ask James for more advice. He seems like the kind of guy who has no trouble getting dates, and he married a much younger woman, so he must be good at seduction too. But as I lead Vanessa out of the dining hall, I realize I can't ask a man I hardly know for advice of this kind, not again.

When I'd kissed Vanessa by the waterfall, she had enjoyed it. I could tell. But I shouldn't have done that right after her boy toy walked away. No wonder she was upset afterward. I need to rewind and start over. How hard can that be?

In the lobby, Vanessa stops and turns toward me. "Think I'll go for a walk along the beach. See you later."

I grasp her arm when she starts to walk away. "I could go with you. Walking is more fun with a friend."

With a friend who wants to fuck you. That's the part I left out.

She gives me another tight smile. "I'd like to be alone for a while."

"Uh, sure. I get it." What else can I say? I'll sound like a dick if I push to go with her.

I watch her walk out the door and head across the big patio.

Once she has disappeared into the woods, I struggle with my conscience for about ten seconds. Then I hurry outside and trot down the path until I can see Vanessa up ahead. Then I slow down to a normal pace. Don't want her to catch me following. I feel like I've turned into a lecherous twenty-five-year-old, stalking the girl I desperately want to sleep with. I keep Vanessa in sight, just far enough away that I can reasonably claim I'm not stalking her if anyone should ask.

Right. Because people so often ask a naked man if he's stalking his ex-wife.

On this island, I doubt anyone would notice. Everyone's naked here.

I halt at the edge of the beach. Vanessa is wandering down the shore, wearing only the little purse-like thing that holds her phone and drapes crosswise over her chest, as well as a pair of sunglasses. Her hair glistens in the sunshine, and a slight smile curves her lips as if she's completely contented. When she disappears behind a stand of mangrove trees, I go through the woods to trail after her, remaining close to the shore but far enough away that I won't disturb her. She finds a nice stretch of beach beyond the mangroves and stops to admire the scenery. Her smile stretches a bit wider, forming sweet little dimples in her cheeks.

And I get a lump in my throat. She's perfect, and I was an idiot to leave her.

Vanessa removes her phone from her purse and sets it on the ground. Then she seems to remember something and kneels to grab a small bottle out of the purse. I recognize that bottle. I've seen ones exactly like it in the terracotta bowls at the resort, so I know they hold sunscreen.

While she flicks the bottle's cap up and squeezes white cream onto her palm, I move closer and sidle up to a palm tree. She casually spreads the sunscreen over her shoulders, arms, and chest, then bends over to treat her legs. She spreads the cream over her face and neck too, but when she tries to cover her back, she can't quite reach all of it. Being a teacher, though, she figures out a way around that problem. She picks up a palm leaf that had fallen onto the sand, then uses it to finish covering her back.

Her smarts had always turned me on. Today is no different. My dick starts to firm up. But when she saunters out into the gentle swells and turns in a circle with her eyes shut and that smile still on her lips, my dick doesn't need to firm up anymore. I'm hard now. Hard and ready for action.

Vanessa dives into the deeper water. She swims a little ways out and then flips onto her back to float and let the swells push her gradually toward the shore. Her tits capture my attention. I want to race out there and join her among the swells, but I can't move. The vision of her has transfixed me.

I've never been a poet, but watching my ex-wife frolicking in the ocean might turn me into one. I've never actually used the word frolic before, not even in my own thoughts. Her sex appeal is melting my brain.

While I've been fixated on her tits, she floated closer to the shore. Now, she stands up and lowers her body under the water until even her head disappears from view. Then, she erupts out of the swells and stands there while she brushes her soaked hair away from her face and shoulders. She squeezes the excess out of her hair as she ambles back onto the shore.

Vanessa wet and shimmering, hips swaying, tits swinging... It's the most erotic thing I've ever seen.

She ambles over to a palm tree a little ways from the one I'm hiding behind and leans back against it. I creep closer, walking carefully so my footfalls won't disturb her. She closes her eyes. The serenity in her expression gives me a different kind of sensation that has nothing to do with lust. I've never seen her look this way before. I wish I'd been the one to give her that feeling, but I can't change the past.

I come up behind the tree that she's leaning against. "Enjoying the tropical sunshine?"

She jumps and whirls around to frown at me. "What are you doing, Craig? You scared the hell out of me."

"If I scared the hell out of you, that means all that's left is heaven."

Her forehead wrinkles. "Are you drunk?"

"No." I walk out from behind the tree. "Let's make love, Nessa."

"Excuse me? You can't blurt that out like it's a given that I want you."

"You liked it when we kissed yesterday. Loved it, I'd say."

She sets her hands on her hips. "That was a whim. It doesn't mean I want you back."

"But you want me." I move closer and gaze into her beautiful eyes. "You came to a naughty nudist resort. That means you want to get naughty, so let's do it together. No strings."

"That would be much too complicated. We have history, not all of it good."

I lay my palms on her upper arms and glide them up and down slowly, rewarded by the way her breathing grows more labored. "I'm talking about sex, Nessa. Hot, breathtaking sex. I know you want me, and I sure as hell want you."

"We can't. It's crazy."

"But the idea turns you on." I slide one hand over her shoulder and down to her breast. Then I flick my thumb over the taut nipple, making her suck in a sharp breath. "Come on, admit it. You're so turned on that I bet you're already wet for me."

"I'm post-menopausal. That means getting wet usually involves lube."

"Not this time." I move that hand down to her hip and spread my fingers in the hairs on her mound. "Let's find out if I'm right."

She bites her lip hard.

I push my longest finger between her folds.

And she gasps.

I pull my finger out and slide it between my lips, tasting her cream. "You're aroused and wet, Nessa. That means you want me. Just admit it. You want us to fuck right here on the beach where anyone might stumble onto us. I'll let you be on top if that's what turns you on. I'll do anything you want."

She chews on her lip for a moment, and I can tell she's weighing her options. Deny that she wants me just to prove a point, or give in and enjoy a post-menopausal fuck on the beach.

Finally, she releases her lip and sighs. "I do want you, but this has nothing to do with our relationship. We aren't getting back together. This is hot divorced-couple sex, nothing more."

"Whatever you want, Nessa."

"If you want to get inside me today, stop calling me 'Nessa.' It's too intimate."

"Sex is intimate. You can't get away from that." But I can tell she's on the verge of losing interest, which means I need to get us back on track. So, I cup her breast and flick my thumbnail over the tip. The way her lips fall open, I know she still wants to do this. "I want to take you up against this tree, out in the open, and fuck you so thoroughly that you'll see stars. But first, I need to make you come with my mouth on your clit."

She drags her tongue over her bottom lip, doing it so slowly that watching her do that makes my dick twitch. Then she grasps my hard-on, and I know we will be getting it on right here, right now. "I've always loved your dick. The way it feels, the way it tastes, the way you fill me up when we have sex."

I lower myself inch by inch until my knees touch the sand and my face hovers in front of her mound. She used to trim those hairs—for hygienic reasons, she said—but now she has let them grow out to show off their curly nature. I love that. Vanessa has gone wild in more ways than one. And that makes me crave her so deeply that I know I'll never want any other woman.

With two fingers, I gently spread her lips to reveal the sweet, glistening pink flesh between her thighs. "Spread your legs for me a bit. That's perfect." I nuzzle her mound to tease those hairs, and she slaps her palms on the tree, her fingers curling slightly. "Damn, you smell good. Like honey and vanilla with a hint of cinnamon. Those are all things you ate at breakfast this morning, aren't they? I remember how your cream always tasted like mint when we had sex in the evening, because you drank spearmint tea after dinner."

"Oh God, Craig," she moans, though not in a sexy way. "Shut up and do me."

She used to love my dirty talk, but I guess discussing what she eats isn't the right move in this moment. It's been a long time since I tasted Vanessa, and I'm probably overcompensating.

I separate her folds a little more so I can blow a delicate stream of air onto her swollen flesh. Vanessa gasps. *Bingo.* We're back on track now. I drop soft little kisses on her inner thigh while I trace my fingertips up and down her folds, careful to take it slow and give her time to experience all the sensations. Her back arches, lifting those gorgeous tits. I raise my head to swirl my tongue in her navel, and a scratching sound lets me know she just scraped her nails over the tree bark. The aroma of her surrounds me and inundates my senses. After years of not touching her, not tasting her, not feeling her body wrapped around me, I almost can't believe this is really happening.

But it is happening. And I won't skimp on the heat.

"Do me a favor, Vanessa. Take your tits in your hands and massage them while I make you come."

She cups her breasts and begins to massage them in an easy, sensual rhythm.

And my dick throbs again. So, I kiss a path down her belly, from her navel to her mound, and nuzzle those hairs. Then I push my face between her folds and latch on to her stiff clitoris. It's just as firm as I remember, and that means she's ready for me. I close my mouth around that nub and suckle it, gently at first, then increasing the pace and the pressure until she lets out a half-strangled cry and arches her back.

God, she's beautiful in the throes. She's always beautiful, but the intensity of her arousal gives her a glow I can't describe, and I almost wish I could freeze this moment. But I need to watch her come.

I slide one finger into her sheath, curling it to pet her inner walls.

She cries out, her head thrown back, and clutches my head with both hands.

While she undulates her hips, I slide another finger inside her. Spreading those fingers wide, I find I can caress two different spots, both of which drive her wild. She starts panting, and her mouth falls open even while her eyes drift partway closed. Vanessa watches me with her gaze hooded, her attention riveted to what I'm doing. I release her clit and pull my fingers free, then plaster my mouth to her opening and plunge my tongue in as far as it will go, swirling it round and round.

"Oh God, Craig, don't stop, that feels—" Her long, throaty moan emerges in sharp bursts. She seems incapable of finishing whatever she'd been about to say.

I don't care if she never speaks again. The look on her face tells me everything. While I keep thrusting my tongue inside her, I reach up to pinch her clit.

And she explodes, like a star about to go supernova, her orgasm hot and fierce and all-consuming. Her scream echoes off the trees. Her body folds in on itself, and she seems like she'll topple over onto me.

I pick her up and lay her down on the sand. "We'll finish this on the ground. I'm going to make you come again, and I don't care who hears you screaming. We aren't finished yet, Nessa."

Chapter Seven

Craig has never been like this before, not in all the years we were married, and I can't deny one simple fact. He's a sex god. Why did he hide that side of himself for so long? I can ask him that later. Right now, I can't think about anything except how incredible it will feel to have him inside me, this new version who drives me insane with pleasure.

He hovers over me on all fours, bracketing my body, and gazes at me as if he's never seen me naked before, like he can't believe I'm actually lying here beneath him. Then he freezes. "Shit. I don't have a condom."

"I've gone through menopause already. Forget the condom and just keep fucking me, please."

"Anything for you, Nessa."

He shouldn't be calling me that, but I won't criticize him for it right now. I need him inside me like I've never needed anything before.

Craig lies down on top of me, careful not to crush me. He brushes wet hair away from my face, gazing at me with an expression I've never seen before, lust and sweetness and determination all mixed up together. He kisses me softly, then paints a trail down my throat with his lips. I can't stop myself from running my hands up and down his back while he takes my earlobe between his teeth and licks it gently. The tenderness of everything he does makes my heart pound and my breaths quicken, almost like I could come just from what he's doing now.

Then he pushes up onto his elbows, pulls his hips back, and thrusts inside me so languorously that my heart thrashes like it wants to leap out of my chest. I can't make any sound except the faint whispering of my breaths that flutter his hair. He buries his face against my throat while he keeps thrusting slowly, like we have the rest of eternity to draw out the pleasure until we both melt into each other.

He presses his mouth to my ear. "Tell me what you want, Nessa. Slow and sensual, hot and hard, or something else."

"I love this, what you're doing now, but..." I can't believe what I'm about to say, because I couldn't have dreamed I would speak the words. "Fuck me hard, Craig, please."

He rises to into a kneeling position, grasps my knees, and lays them over his shoulders. Then he drops onto all fours as he plunges inside me so deeply that I swear I can feel his cock nudging my cervix. That's impossible, since I had a total hysterectomy years ago and no longer have a cervix. But my brain insists that's what I'm feeling, and I'm too far gone to give a damn about reality. I grip his biceps while he pulls almost all the way out, teasing me with with tip of his erection, and finally starts to fuck me the way I'd begged him to do. He punches into me over and over, grunting with every inward lunge, thrusting hard and deep, making me bounce and my tits jiggle.

The suction created by our bodies makes a wet sound that turns me on even more. I'm so aroused that it's almost painful, and I need to come like I've never needed it before, but I don't want this to end. My dueling needs to come and to stave it off trigger desperate noises that burst out of me in the most embarrassing way. I throw my hands above my head and arch my back, sinking my fingers into the warm sand.

Craig circles his hips while he keeps thrusting forcefully, and that motion pushes me over the edge. I tumble off the cliff, my inner muscles pulsating around his cock as my body tenses and fasten my hands on his upper arms. The pleasure steals my breath away. I can't even scream, though my mouth falls open, and my legs fold toward my chest.

He thrusts one more time, holding that position, while his face contorts and a strangled shout bursts out of him. Then he drops onto the sand beside me, on his back, breathing hard. "Was that good for you?"

I turn my head to squint at him, ready to complain about his statement. But then I notice that he's smirking. So instead of bitching, I elbow him in the side. "Very funny. But that wasn't 'good.' It was incredible."

"Yeah, it was hands-down the best we've ever been."

"Why didn't we have sex like this before?"

"I guess divorce makes it hotter."

Maybe it does, but I'd rather not discuss that topic anymore. The lingering tingle between my thighs and the fact that my whole body still feels hypersensitized means I need to change the subject now. One touch of his pinky finger could push me over the edge again.

I wriggle to create some distance between our bodies. "Thank you for that. I needed it. But this was one time, and we will never do it again. Agreed?"

"No, I don't agree. You can't expect me to forget about the incredible sex we had on the beach like it never happened."

"Don't get grumpy with me. I never said we should pretend it didn't happen." I sit up and start brushing the sand off my arms. "Let's just think of this as a nice memory and a final goodbye to our marriage."

"We're stuck on this island together for two weeks. Naked. At a resort that puts out bowls of condoms for the guests." He sits up too, planting one hand on the sand between us, and leans toward me. "Now that I know our chemistry is better than ever, I can't give up on us."

"Sex is not a reliable gauge for our compatibility." I jump up and brush off more sand, though there are some places on my body that I can't clean up without taking a shower. "Please don't make this a big deal, Craig. It was great, but it's over now."

"You've got sand all over your backside too. Better take a dip in the ocean."

Though I hate to admit it, he's right. I can't clean off my backside myself, and I sure as hell won't ask him to do that for me. I'm still too turned on. Before Craig can get any ideas about sweeping the sand off my back, I jog out into the water and plunge under the surface. Just as I spring up again, Craig dives into the swells too and emerges a moment later, grinning at me.

Oh no, I recognize that smile. He wants to seduce me again. This island has clearly affected him in strange ways, turning my laid-back ex into an insatiable beast.

He shakes his head, sending droplets of water raining down on me. "How about lunch? I'm famished."

"You go on. I think I'll order room service."

"That's a great idea. We can talk while we eat."

I stand up, which means half of me is still submerged. "No, Craig, I'm having lunch alone in my suite. 'Alone' means by myself, solo, unaccompanied."

He sighs and stands up. His dick emerges from the water every time a swell breaks and subsides. "You always were stubborn. Fine, go eat alone in your suite."

"Thank you for the permission I didn't need." Did I sound bitchy? That wasn't my intention, but he's driving me crazy. I feel like a college girl on spring break, trying to fend off horny young men. "I'm sorry. That came out wrong. But I honestly do just want to eat in my room."

"Sure, I understand." He strides out of the water and waits on the beach until I reach him. Then he gives me a forlorn smile. "See you around."

He walks into the woods and vanishes from my sight.

I hurt his feelings, though I never wanted to do that. What we just did here on this beach has left me so confused that I need to get away from everyone for a little while. So, I head back to my room and, fortunately, don't see Craig along the way. I don't see Zach either, thank goodness. He's a sweet kid, but I can't deal with men's feelings right now.

Once I've stepped inside my suite, I lean back to push the door closed with my body—and then I sag against it, my eyes shut. How did a naughty vacation turn into an angsty mess? I'm too damn old for that, but here I am stuck in the middle.

I order a ridiculous amount of food. Luckily, a woman delivers my meal, so I don't need to contend with any men for a while. Nothing has ever tasted as good as the delicacies I'm devouring right now, but I have a feeling that's in part an aftereffect of the beach incident. I always get ravenous after sex. Of course, I haven't done the deed with anyone in a long time, not until today, so that fact might have heightened my hunger too.

For food. Not for my ex-husband.

After lunch, I decide to join an outing organized by the resort staff. We're on the hunt for exotic wildlife and plants. Our guide is Emilio Rocha, the assistant manager. He's attractive and very nice, with a voice that's perfect for this kind of job. He clearly knows his stuff too. Most of the people in the tour group are couples, except for a small cadre of twenty-something men. I wind up walking alongside Emilio, who doesn't seem to mind at all. In between telling us about the flowers and birds, he keeps me company. I don't think he does that because he feels sorry for me. He seems like the type who's friendly to everyone.

Experiencing the ecosystem on this island is fascinating, but I keep flashing back to the beach and Craig.

We hike to the far end of the main beach, where Emilio tells us about the fish and other aquatic wonders. But my mind starts to wander again, returning to the beach, replaying those moments with Craig and the way he'd made me feel. But that's the past. *He* is my past. Why, then, can't I stop thinking about what we did?

"Look!" Emilio shouts. "There are two dolphins."

Everyone clamors to get a good look, but I don't even glance in that direction.

"You all right, Vanessa?" Emilio asks. "You look a bit sick."

I shake off the memories and clear my throat. "No, I'm fine. I zoned out for a minute, that's all."

"But you missed the dolphins."

"Maybe I'll catch them another time."

"It's none of my business, but I, ah, can't help wondering..."

Why I'm alone when my ex is here on the island. That seems like the logical end for that sentence. Emilio is too polite to finish his statement. What the hell? Might as well confess. "You're wondering why I'm not hanging out with Craig instead of going on a nature hike by myself."

"Yeah. You two seem to get on well enough."

"We do, usually. But I had no idea he would be here, and his arrival threw me off kilter."

"I get it. Sorry. I shouldn't have pestered you."

"You haven't done that." I pat his arm. "You're a terrific tour guide and assistant manager."

He smiles. "Thank you for the compliment. But my job is to make sure everyone is comfortable, having a good time, and enjoying their stay. Feel like I've failed with you."

"Don't worry about me. I think I'm just having trouble figuring out what to do with myself. I haven't taken a vacation in years, maybe decades."

"I hear that a lot from guests." He puckers his lips, apparently thinking hard about something. Me, probably. Then he raises one finger and grins. "I've got it. We're having a masquerade ball tomorrow night. All the guests will wear face masks and body-paint costumes. Doesn't that sound like fun?"

He really is determined to make me enjoy life. I can't say no. "Yeah, that could be fun. I've never done anything like that, for sure."

"Brilliant. And in the meantime, there will be miniten matches on the south lawn. And I'll be taking a small group to Suva for some shopping. Why don't you participate in all of those events? It would distract you for sure."

What the heck? At least Craig won't be there. He was never a fan of shopping. "That all sounds great, Emilio. Thank you." I kiss his cheek. "You are the best assistant manager I've ever met."

He blushes. "Thanks, Vanessa."

Once we return to the resort proper, I head for the miniten court to find out more about the game, since I'd only casually observed a match. Holly Bythesea comes over to me and offers to explain the basics of miniten before I attempt to participate in a match. Players follow the rules of tennis, mostly, though Holly informs me that nobody enforces those rules. Guests come here to relax, after all, not engage in official sporting events. The thugs players use instead of rackets baffle me. Who on earth came up with the idea of putting a box around the player's hand?

Holly laughs. "Yeah, it is weird. Miniten was invented in the nineteen thirties to accommodate the quirks of the naturist lifestyle. Most resorts don't have enough land to create a regulation tennis court, so smaller ones became the norm. Now, it's become a tradition, and there's even a book outlining the rules. We sell that book in the gift shop."

"Interesting. I might need to buy a copy."

Zach jogs up to us, though he's focused on me, not Holly, though she's much closer to his age than I am. "Hey, Vanessa. Want to play a little miniten with us? My partner left to take a class on creating shell necklaces. I need a new partner. What do you say?"

Oh, what the hell. I can't reasonably avoid Zach for the entire two weeks we're here. "I'd love to do that. After seeing how you play the game, I have no doubts you'll be a great miniten coach for a newbie like me."

"Awesome." He offers me his arm. "Let me escort you onto the court."

Zach has shattered all my preconceptions about people in their twenties. He might say "awesome" sometimes, but he's a true gentleman.

I let him lead me out onto the miniten court, which is just a well-mown grassy area. Lawn chairs and chaises have been set up at the periphery so that spectators can comfortably watch the matches. Small tables positioned here and there between the chairs have umbrellas attached to them. I see some of the people I'd met on the nature walk sitting there watching, waiting for the next match to begin.

Holly had explained some of the rules to me, but Zach tells me that we need a strategy to win, otherwise we will "get our asses wiped like newborn babies." I can't help laughing at that. He doesn't seem irritated that I found his statement amusing. Instead, he grins.

Then the match begins.

Our opponents are a man and a woman who seem to be about my age. Is it fair to have middle-aged people competing against a muscular young man? Well, I will probably be a hindrance for our side, since I've never played miniten before. But the couple on the other side of the net seem like they're pros. To me, a miniten pro is anyone who has played the game at least once. I doubt anyone here is a true pro, and I'm pretty sure there isn't a professional miniten league. This seems like a game for amateurs.

I've just hit the ball over the net with my thug for the first time when someone whoops.

"Go, Nessa!"

Those three syllables make me freeze and slowly rotate my head toward the man who had shouted that encouragement. I swear every hair on my body stiffens as if an electrical current has arced over my skin.

Craig gives me the thumbs-up sign.

A tingle of excitement sweeps through me as a memory of our time on the beach explodes in my mind. And I know what that means.

Oh, shit. I want to screw my ex-husband again.

Chapter Eight

Craig

Why is Vanessa gaping at me that way? I was trying to be nice and show support for her first attempt at playing miniten. My ex-wife had never been a fan of sports, though she always loved watching our son Greg play baseball when he was high school. Vanessa would whoop and jump up and down, clapping so hard that I think her palms must have been sore afterward. She never participated in sports, though.

Until today. She seems to love miniten.

Maybe that's because her horny young suitor is playing by her side.

No, I'm not jealous. I'm too old for that shit. But I'd hoped that our interlude on the beach would have changed something between us. Shouldn't making love on the sand on a tropical island have brought us closer together? But no, she seems even more determined to run away from me.

She's scared. I understand that, considering the fact that *I* divorced *her*. The only way I can win her back is if I tell her everything, but I doubt she'll listen—unless I can prove to her that I'm serious about rekindling our relationship. That might be an impossible task, but I won't give up. Vanessa Stendahl has been the love of my life since the day we met. I know she still uses her married name, even though we're divorced, and I don't care that she added her maiden name in there to become Vanessa Stendahl Hathaway. She could rename herself Mrs. Santa Claus and I wouldn't care.

Vanessa finally stops gaping at me and faces the net again.

I can't get over how silly those thugs are. A wedge-shaped wooden box? On your hand? Naturists are crazy. But I can't deny I love watching Vanessa whack the ball with her thug. She jumps up to do that, and her tits flap wildly. When she realizes the other team failed to hit the ball, and she and Zach have won the match, Vanessa flings her arms up and whoops.

Then she spins around and throws herself at Zach.

My fingers clench, my jaw too. She has her naked body plastered to that kid, plastered to his dick. I shouldn't be jealous, I know that. She's just happy to have won the match. I force myself to relax and clap for the winning team, since I don't want to come across as a stalker. I love that woman, and I will do anything to get her back.

Vanessa finally peels her body away from Zach's. She kisses his cheek.

And then she walks toward me.

But she doesn't sit down on the chair beside mine. She stands there, hands on her hips, and studies me. "Thanks for the cheers. I appreciate your support during the miniten match."

"You're welcome. Can't believe how fast you took to the game."

She shrugs. "Holly gave me a brief primer on miniten, and Zach showed me a few things too."

"That was an impressive backhand, especially since you were wearing a wedge on your hand."

She nods toward the glass of ice water on the table beside me. "Mind if I drink some? I need a little refreshment before I head back onto the court."

I hand her the glass. "Be my guest. So, you're playing another match?"

With the young stud who has the hots for you. That's the part I omitted.

"Yes, I am going another round." She gulps the water, then sets the glass down, leaning over so her tits dangle in my face. "But I need a new partner. Zach is heading off to a yoga class. Are you game for trying miniten?"

I stare at her, sure I misunderstood what she said or that I'm hallucinating, maybe both. But no, she's serious. I focus on her face, not those gorgeous globes that keep swaying right in front of me. "Sure, I'd love to give miniten a go."

"Great. Do you know the rules?"

"I, uh, kind of read a book about it while I was having lunch alone in my suite. They sell that book in the gift shop."

She straightens. "Yeah, I know. Holly told me about it. Are you ready to play?"

Yes, I would love to play with Vanessa in every sense of the word. But I know she means one thing and one thing only. "Let's whup some youngsters' asses and show them how old farts get it done."

Vanessa peers around my chair. "Don't see your walker. Did you forget and leave it in your suite?"

"Ha-ha." It's embarrassing how happy I feel just because she teased me. I want to kiss her, but I'll ruin this new camaraderie between us if I do that. "Come on, let's rock the miniten court."

She smiles with her lips sealed, and the cutest dimples form in her cheeks. My ex-wife leads me out onto the grass court, where another couple waits on the other side. It's a different couple than the two people who had played against Vanessa and Zach. These guys look like they just graduated from high school last week. Of course, I'm an old fart, so everyone under forty seems like a child to me.

I'm hardly an expert on miniten, but I've learned enough to know it's a lot like tennis. Miniten is supposed to be more laid-back, and the court is considerably smaller. But I haven't seen any evidence that it really is an easygoing sport. I watched Zach and Vanessa whacking that ball like they wanted to knock a tree down with it. I suppose the people here play hard because this is a very naughty nudist resort. It's not the family-friendly kind.

Vanessa picks up the thug Zach had left on the court and offers it to me. Then she shows me how to put it over my hand. This thing feels weird. I have to hold on to a bar inside the wedge-shaped box. Vanessa picks up her thug to show me how to use it, as if she's an expert on the subject after one match. Well, she is an expert compared to me.

Our competitors, a husband and wife who just got married a week ago, make the first serve. They have youthful stamina on their side, so I expect Vanessa and I will lose this match. She can handle it, as her first match proved, but I'm a newbie who has never touched any kind of racket in my life. I never observed a tennis match either. Watching a ball go back and forth across the net had never seemed exciting or even interesting to me.

But right now, I can't stop watching Vanessa hit that ball. We're taking it easy, the way miniten is supposed to be, so I don't get to watch her tits bouncing as much as they had when she smashed that ball to win the match earlier. I'm happy just to watch her movements, the easy way she serves, her graceful manner of hitting the ball whenever it comes her way. She kept her hair loose, and I love the way it flies up when she whacks that ball, then falls over her shoulders again.

I've never seen anything more beautiful.

Well, except for the way she looks when she comes.

After five minutes or so, I start to get into the game a bit more. Watching Vanessa had done more than get me turned on. It helped me get the hang of miniten. Sure, I also watched our opposing couple. But Vanessa has more finesse on the court than either of them—or me.

Now that I'm in the groove, I strike the ball the next time it comes our way and send it sailing over the net. My young opponent misses the ball and shakes his head, but he doesn't seem genuinely upset about screwing up.

He grins at me. "Hey, old man! Wanna see who craps out first?"

"You're a baby. That means you'll crap first—in your diaper."

"Betcha five bucks Elaine and me win."

"Five dollars? Come on. Be a man and bet me ten bucks."

"You're on, old man."

Elaine shakes her head at her husband. "I don't know, Tim. Craig looks really fit. You think a workout means carrying a twelve-pack of beer into the kitchen."

Tim rolls his eyes at his wife, then smirks at me. "You're in for it now, old man. It's your turn to serve."

I toss the ball up in the air, then smack it with my thug. The ball goes sailing over the next, heading straight for the whippersnapper who thinks I'm an old man. Tim hits the ball, but it lands in the net.

"Don't feel bad," I call out to Tim. "I'll give you a baby serve this time. Maybe we should use a Nerf ball for the rest of the game."

He kicks the ball with his big toe, and it rolls across the well-mown grass, halting a couple of feet away from me.

I snag it and assume the appropriate stance. "Ready this time, pipsqueak?"

Tim gets in position. "Oh, yeah. Let's do it."

As the match resumes, Tim hits the ball over the net, and Vanessa sends it flying back onto the other side of the court. Elaine swings her thug up to hurl the ball back to me. I whack it, and though I hadn't meant to do it, I make the thing go over the net at a downward trajectory that neither Tim nor Elaine could move fast enough to catch.

Our match goes on for a little longer. By the time it's over, nobody really remembers who won or lost. At least, I don't remember. Keeping score didn't seem all that important.

Tim trots around the net and holds out his hand to me. "You guys were awesome. Didn't know old people could move that fast."

I make a sarcastically infuriated face. "Careful what you say about my ex-wife. I might need to corner you in the woods and toss you into the waterfall."

He laughs. "You're pretty cool for an old guy."

I finally shake his hand. "You're pretty cool too, kid. And you know old people like me were using the word cool long before your generation learned how to spell it."

He grins and slaps my arm. "Maybe we could have a rematch sometime."

"Whenever you want."

Tim and Elaine amble away from the lawn, disappearing around the corner of the resort building.

I turn to Vanessa. "That was fun. Who knew naked tennis could be such a good time?"

She stares at me with a strange expression. "You actually enjoyed playing sports, didn't you?"

"Miniten isn't just any sport. It's unusual."

"But *you* played sports. When Greg was on the high school football team, you didn't like having to go to the games. You said they were boring."

"Football is boring. I'm a baseball guy, you know that. I never let on to our son that I hate his favorite sport. I cheered just like you did."

Her brows wrinkle. She shakes her head slowly. "I don't understand you at all anymore."

"Because I had a good time playing miniten? You were enjoying yourself too."

"Yes, but—Never mind." She offers me her hand like she wants to shake it. "Congratulations. We won the match."

This might be the most bizarre conversation I've ever had with my ex-wife. I accept her hand, but I don't shake it. Instead, I raise her hand to my lips and kiss it. "Congratulations to you too, Nessa. We beat those whippersnappers good."

She wriggles her hand free of mine. "Maybe we can play another match sometime. Have a good evening."

Evening? It's still afternoon. I guess that's her way of telling me that she doesn't want to see me again today. But she invited me to play miniten with her. Maybe she's in denial about wanting to spend time with me. Or maybe I'm so desperate to get back in her good graces that I'm imagining she feels what I feel. As she walks away, one thought consumes me. I will love that woman until the day I die and after that too, until the universe explodes and nothing is left but a cloud of cosmic dust.

Too bad I didn't realize that a few years ago.

I spend the rest of the afternoon in my suite, watching TV shows from Fiji, New Zealand, Australia, and several Asian countries. The latter shows don't have subtitles, and I don't speak any of the languages in those series. I guess the owners of the resort thought guests would enjoy experiencing the cultures of this region of the world. I'm old and set in my ways, though, which means I'd rather be watching an American baseball game.

Being around all those nubile young people makes me feel like I'm a thousand years old.

I'm just getting into a New Zealand mystery show when the screen turns to snow. I wait a few minutes, but the picture doesn't come back. I wait a few more minutes, then give up and turn off the TV. I guess that was the universe's way of ordering me to go outside and get some fresh air.

After a brief walk, I decide to get a snack in the dining hall. But as I'm entering the lobby, I notice a sign that hadn't been there before. It's large and rectangular, and it sits on a metal easel. But it's what the sign says that catches my attention and makes me halt a few feet away from the easel. I stare at the words.

Masquerade party tomorrow night, the sign says. *Body paint costumes only, choose your own mask. Party starts at 8pm.*

What kind of costumes? I don't understand the sign, so I approach the front desk and ask the young woman who's posted there. Her name tag identifies her as Marley. I clear my throat. "Uh, what is a body paint costume?"

"Guests are naked all the time, so we can't have regular fancy dress. Holly had the idea of everyone wearing costumes made of body paint."

"I still don't understand. Body paint?"

Marley laughs, but it's not mockery. She seems to think my confusion is charming. "Your costume will be sprayed onto your body with special paint. It's edible."

"What is edible?"

"The body paint." She hands me a brochure. "This explains everything about the masquerade party. If you have any more questions, please ask Emilio. He and Holly set up the party and know all the details. We're bringing in an expert from Sydney to create the costumes."

I take the brochure. "Thanks, Marley."

While I make my way to the dining hall for that snack I'd wanted, I flip the brochure open and skim the information. It includes photos of people wearing body paint costumes, though a note underneath the pictures advises that these are examples photos only. The resort has never hosted a party like this one before. The body paint costumes run the gamut from a sprayed-on tuxedo to fantasy creatures. Some costumes cover the face.

Marley had said they're bringing in an expert to paint us all up. I can't deny I'm intrigued by the possibilities of body paint.

Edible paint? That intrigues me even more.

I bump into someone and mumble an apology, too absorbed by the possibilities of a body paint costume party to notice what's going on around me. Even while I'm in the dining hall, eating a slice of key lime pie, I keep reading and re-reading the brochure. Edible paint. I can't stop thinking about that. My mind conjures visions of Vanessa wearing a sprayed-on costume and a mask. I imagine walking up to her, dancing with her, whispering in her ear that I'd relish the chance to lick off all that paint.

My dick loves the idea.

But will Vanessa go for it? She claims she doesn't want to have sex with me ever again, but on that beach, she begged me to make her come. I know I've never been great at seducing women. Never had much call to do that. Everything with Vanessa had been easy, until the day it wasn't.

Will edible body paint change things between us? I'll find out tomorrow night.

Chapter Nine

Vanessa

I wake up in the morning feeling terrific. I slept well, so I must have recovered from the jet lag by now. But I had the strangest dreams all night long. Strangely hot dreams. In those fantasies, a mysterious man sneaked into my bed and made love to me in the most erotic ways, pushing me to climax after climax, and I kept begging for more, hungry to experience that man's body until we both collapsed. That wasn't the strange part of the dream. No, the weird part was the man's identity.

My dream lover was Craig.

That doesn't mean I want to get back together with him. Dreams aren't literal. So, my naughty fantasy probably just means that being on this island where everyone is naked all the time has affected me. I love it here on Heirani Motu. I've never felt freer or more alive than I do now. Over the years, I'd forgotten how to enjoy the sensual side of life.

I lie in bed for a while after waking up, just to enjoy the silky softness of the sheets and the tropical breeze that wafts into my room. I'd left the patio doors open. Why lock myself in overnight? I'm at a private resort. Maybe the breeze and the scent of the flowers on the patio caused my sensual dream last night. It couldn't have anything to do with Craig.

He wants me back. But even if I wanted to reconcile, we're too old to start over again.

I stretch my entire body and sigh. The sheets really are the softest I've ever felt. The sensation of that silk trailing over my skin makes me horny. Well, I'm a grown woman who knows how to take care of urges like that. I hop out of bed and saunter into the bathroom to switch on the multiple showerheads. Once the temperature is just right, I step into the stall and shut the glass door. Steam gathers around me. I turn my back to the wall and tip my head back to let the steamy water engulf me. As I comb my fingers through my hair, a memory of that dream slips into my mind.

Craig licking every inch of my body. Craig devouring my cream. Craig thrusting into me while he seals his mouth over mine for a deep kiss.

Oh, shit. Why can't I stop thinking about that damn dream? And why is it getting me so turned on? The fact that I'm aroused because of a dream that involved my ex-husband doesn't mean I want him back. But this once, strictly to eradicate my growing arousal, I give in and fantasize about Craig.

My fantasy begins casually, with Craig gliding his hands over my entire body, taking his time to explore every inch of me. While the water sluices over me, I close my eyes and run my hands over my skin in the same way Craig had done in my steamy dream. *Mm, this feels so good.* I cup my breasts and massage them, picturing him the entire time, even as I slide one hand down to my mound and push two fingers between my folds.

A deep, hungry moan spills from my lips.

Craig urging me to spread my legs. Craig latching on to my clit and suckling it like he'll die without the flavor of me on his tongue.

I rub myself with those two fingers and sag against the wall while the water continues to rain down on me. With one hand, I pinch my nipple. With the other, I rub my clit, heightening my need until I can't hold back anymore. Visions of Craig take over my mind, and I can't think about anything else except hitting that climax. My moans grow louder, echoing off the shower walls, while I begin to gasp and rub myself faster and harder.

The orgasm crashes through me so powerfully that my knees buckle, and I grasp the showerhead to keep from falling down. A strangled cry erupts out of me. Pleasure courses through me, stealing my breath. Even once the orgasm has faded, I still feel hypersensitized and struggle to catch my breath. For a moment, I lean against the wall and just let myself come down from the high. But the DIY kind of pleasure can't match how it had felt when Craig went down on me on the beach and then took my body too.

No, I will not think about that anymore. So what if I got off while picturing him going down on me? It was a fantasy, not reality.

I finish my shower and step out of the stall. But just as I'm reaching for the hair dryer, someone knocks on the door to my suite. I hurry out there to pull the door open, wet hair and all.

Craig eyes me up and down, then smirks. "Good morning, Nessa. You look fresh and wet, just the way I like you best."

"I've asked you more than once to please stop calling me Nessa. We aren't married anymore."

"Nobody knows you better than I do."

"Really." I fold my arms over my chest. "Then why don't you know that I mean it when I say we are never getting back together?"

He sighs, leaning against the jamb. "Come on, chill out. Let's have breakfast outdoors this morning. Like a picnic."

Why does he insist on ignoring everything I say? He told me to "chill out," as if he's a hippie. My ex has never been that sort of man. He's the type who believes in work before play. We never did much playing, actually. We both worked too hard.

"No picnic," I tell him. "We are not dating, Craig. I might have moved out of the house, but you divorced me. End of story."

"Hmm." He gazes directly into my eyes. "Have you heard about the masquerade party? We'll all wear body paint costumes."

"I know. Emilio told me about that."

"Will you be attending the party?" He raises a hand before I can balk. "Not suggesting we should go as a couple. But if you happen to be there, and I happen to be there..."

"You and I might bump into each other. That's all."

"Did you know the body paint will be edible?"

I stare at him. I think my jaw has fallen open too. Edible body paint? That's crazy. Why would anyone want... *Oh, fuck*. He wants to lick that paint off my body, doesn't he? Ever since I arrived on this island, I've felt like a teenager again, or at least a college girl. The mature science teacher kissed a sinfully young man and let her former husband do wicked things to her on the beach.

What is wrong with me?

"Doesn't matter to me that the paint is edible," I say. "Because I don't plan on eating it. Food is the only thing I'll be eating."

He slants closer. "But I could lick it off your body."

"We won't be doing that either. People our age don't do such things."

"You make it sound like we're ninety and need help to use the restroom." He roves his gaze over me from head to toe. "You are not old. You're as hot as the young women on this island. Hotter, actually. There's nothing sexier than a mature woman who knows what she wants."

"Why don't you go flirt with an obscenely young woman? That's what men your age are supposed to do. Besides, I have plans for the day." No, I don't. But sometimes lying is a necessary evil, especially when my ex wants to talk about edible body paint.

Craig pushes away from the jamb. "Sure, I'll go. We'll see each other at the party tonight, anyway."

"Not sure I'm going."

He smirks again, and winks too. "Afraid you can't resist me, hey?"

"No." I push the door halfway closed. "Goodbye. Have fun with the sex kittens."

I shut the door all the way. Then I turn around and lean against it, blowing out a breath. I hope he couldn't tell I was aroused. Never will he ever find out that I got off in the shower while fantasizing about him.

My cell phone rings.

I race over to the nightstand to grab my phone, and I see it's my oldest daughter, Nicole. It must be about sixteen hours later here, but I'm too frazzled to do the math right now. I skip that and say hello. "What's up, sweetie? Is something wrong?"

"We're all fine, Mom. Well, except for Dad. We haven't been able to get ahold of him by phone or email."

"He's fine. Trust me."

Nicole hesitates, then asks, "Why does it sound like you know exactly where he is? You're in the South Pacific."

Craig must not have told anyone that he was flying to Heirani Motu.

"Dad is here with me, Nic."

"Where exactly are you guys? A spontaneous vacation isn't your style, especially since you're divorced."

"It's a long story. But don't worry, we're fine."

She makes little tuneless humming sounds, which always means she's suspicious. "Are you two getting back together?"

"No, absolutely not. Your father... Well, he, um, followed me here."

"What? Dad is stalking you?" Nicole laughs more boisterously than seems appropriate. "That's great, Mom!"

"You think your father is stalking me, and you like the idea? What kind of demented child did we raise?"

"Take a chill pill, Mom. Dad isn't actually a stalker. But I'm glad you guys wound up on the same island, which is called...what? I forgot."

I tsk. "That's because I never told you the island's name."

"Come on. What if there's an emergency? You need to tell us where to go to bring the caskets home."

"That's not funny." I drum my nails on the nightstand, trying to decide how much I should share with my daughter. Nicole is an adult and the mother of a new baby, so I'm sure she can handle the truth. "The resort is on a private island called Heirani Motu that's exclusively for guests of the Au Naturel Naturist Resort South Seas."

"Naturist? You're birdwatching or something?"

I wince, though she can't see that. "No, honey. It's a nudist resort."

Silence. I can hear faint static on the line as I count the seconds until she speaks again. One, two, three, four—

Nicole bursts into a fit of uproarious laughter.

I wait while she gets it out of her system and blows her nose. "You're serious, aren't you? Vanessa and Craig Hathaway are staying at a nudist resort. That means you're both naked, right? Ooh, that's perfect."

"Why is it perfect? I don't like it when you get that sneaky tone in your voice." I won't point out that I go by Stendahl now, not Hathaway. She knows that but chooses to ignore it.

"Of course it's perfect. You and Dad, naked all the time... Oh yeah, that's definitely going to end with you guys tying the knot again."

"Don't get your hopes up. We will not be getting remarried. Your dad and I live separate lives now." I drop my head into my hand. "Except when we both wound up on the same island."

"That's a good thing. He wants you back, Mom, can't you tell? You guys are meant to be together."

"No, we're not."

"We'll see." Nicole makes those humming noises again. "Can I be the one to tell April and Greg?"

Naturally, she sounds like she just can't wait to break the shocking news to her brother and sister.

"Sure, fine, you can tell them." I suddenly get an idea that would be a rotten thing to do to my ex-husband. But he tricked me into coming here, so maybe he deserves a little comeuppance. "And you can tell your dad that I shared our vacation plans with you."

"He'll freak, won't he? Dad is always so calm. It'll be nice to hear him panicking for once."

"Your father will not panic. But his face might turn beet red, like a cartoon character, when he blows his top."

"Ooh, I'll make it a video call."

I glance at the clock on the nightstand. "I should go, sweetie. I have no idea how much an international phone call costs."

"Okay. Talk to you later, Mom." Her tone turns sneaky again. "Have fun with Dad."

I end the call and set my phone on the nightstand. If I don't take it with me today, then Craig will have a harder time finding me. I hope. But no, I shouldn't do that. What if Nicole calls? She'll be worried when I don't answer, so I grab my little phone purse.

Time to find out more about tonight's masquerade party.

Chapter Ten

Craig

Since Vanessa doesn't want to spend time with me this morning, I decide to take my breakfast out onto the smaller patio that's situated near the pool that curves around in snake-like fashion. From here, I have a great view of the ocean. The woods obscure the scenery at my left and right, but I don't mind that. The palms and the flowering flame trees and siris trees provide color. I learned the names of those trees from a book I bought in the gift shop.

I hook one ankle over the opposite knee while I sip my tea and enjoy a light breakfast. Heirani Motu is the most beautiful place I've ever visited. Just gazing out at the scenery makes me feel more relaxed and at peace. A few guests are swimming in the pool. As I watch, two young men come into view, swimming around the sharpest curve in the pool, as if they've come from somewhere around the corner of the building.

Three gorgeous young women amble past me and say hello. But I barely notice them.

"Oh, shit."

I can't help smiling when I hear that curse, hissed under the breath of the one person I want to see this morning. I twist my head around to look at her. "Good morning, Vanessa. Why don't you join me? I could order more food."

She winces. "I was planning to sneak away before you saw me."

"If that was your plan, you shouldn't have cursed under your breath."

"That was an unconscious impulse."

A chuckle rumbles out of me, which is my unconscious response to what she said. "Sometimes those are the best impulses. Your mind is trying to tell you something."

"Like what?" She raises a hand before I can respond. "That was a rhetorical question. I know what you think, but that thing on the beach was a singular mistake."

I point toward the chair across from me. "Why not sit down? I promise not to talk about sex. But it's nice to have someone to talk to, isn't it?"

She bites her lip, studying the table as if it might reach out to grab her. Then she finally sits down.

I hand her a menu.

Vanessa scrutinizes it as if deciding whether to have scrambled eggs or a frittata is the most vital decision she's ever made. I suspect she's just trying to avoid looking at me. One of the resort employees—whose name is Leo, a fact I learned earlier when I ordered my food—comes over and asks if Vanessa wants to order. She glances at me and winces, then nods.

"What can I get for you, ma'am?"

She glances at me. "What did you eat, Craig?"

"I had the traditional Fiji breakfast."

"Okay. I'll have that too."

Leo nods and takes the menu, hustling away to get her order.

Vanessa leans forward and whispers, "What's in the traditional Fiji breakfast?"

"Didn't you read the menu? And why are you whispering?"

"I don't know." She sits back and sighs. "So, what is in the traditional breakfast?"

"You'll like it, I promise. Leo explained it all to me. The meal includes lolo buns, which are a type of bread that's steamed in coconut milk. You also get babakau, a fried thing that's kind of like a cross between a donut and a pancake. Then you've got the scones and pudding, and it's all topped off with draunimoli tea."

"That sounds interesting. You know I love trying the local cuisine, wherever we go."

"I wish we'd traveled more. This is only the second time either of us has ever left the continental United States. At least we made it to Hawaii with the kids."

"Yeah, I know. We were both so busy with our jobs and our kids that we never got around to taking that world tour we used to talk about."

The world tour. We used to dream about doing that, back when we were newlyweds. Once in a while after that, one of us would bring up the idea again, but we gradually stopped dreaming about it. Our kids took precedence, and we worked damn hard to earn a good living so we could give them the best education. I'm proud of Greg, Nicole, and April, and everything they've accomplished. I wouldn't change a thing about my life with Vanessa and the kids. But once they were all grown up and started their own lives, we drifted apart.

I suppose it was the empty nest syndrome.

Once Vanessa's food arrives, she has a great excuse to avoid talking to me. But she doesn't do that. She devours a big hunk of lolo bun, then looks at me. "Do you really regret filing for divorce?"

"Yeah, of course I do. That's why I'm glad we're both here at this resort. I'd like for us to talk about what happened, why our marriage disintegrated."

"We aren't getting back together." She sips her draunimoli tea while she studies me, then sets the cup down. "I think we should have a serious conversation about our marriage, just to set things straight. Our children might be adults now, but they need for us to work out our differences. It will be good for them and for us."

"I agree. We could go to your suite—"

"No. We'll take a walk and discuss things."

The eternally optimistic part of me wants to believe she's afraid she won't be able to keep her hands off me if we have our talk in her suite. But I doubt that's the reason she suggested a walk. At least she's going to talk to me. I need to explain a lot of things too, but I'm not the one who shied away from it yesterday.

She agreed to a conversation. I shouldn't assume that means anything.

Once Vanessa has finished her breakfast, we wander down the nearest path through the woods. I had memorized all the trails last night, when I had nothing else to do because watching TV is the most boring way to spend an evening. My welcome packet included detailed maps of the island. So now, I lead Vanessa into a region I haven't explored yet. I need to fight the impulse to clasp her hand. Decades of holding her hand is a hard habit to break.

"Do you know where you're going?" she asks. "Or are you planning to stop at a random place?"

"I know where I'm going. Pretty much. The resort map shows that this trail goes past several spots where we could sit down to talk."

"Did your data tell you that?"

"No, a map did. For these two weeks, I'm not a data scientist. I'm just a guy on vacation."

"And I'm not a science teacher. Just a woman who needed a getaway."

A colorful bird flies by, and Vanessa grins. She hops up and down too, something I haven't see her do since we were newlyweds. It's the cutest thing. I want to pull her into my arms and kiss her, but I doubt she'd appreciate that.

"What kind of bird was that?" I ask. "You're the science teacher, so I thought you might know."

"I think it was a cockatoo, but I only know that mostly because I went on Emilio's nature hike yesterday. He's a great tour guide. I also started reading a book about the local wildlife."

"Emilio's a good kid. Very smart, but not as smart as you."

We continue walking and finally reach one of the spots I'd found on the map. It's not just a place where there's a clearing in the woods. The resort created this little spot for the guests. A small area on a cliff has been cleared of brush to reveal a stunning view of a beach below and the ocean. The cliff isn't as tall as the mountain that sits at the center of the island, but it does serve as a spectacular overlook.

I sit down first, and Vanessa takes care to sit at the end furthest from me. I've still got a long ways to go to win her back.

"You go first," she says. "The one who broke up our marriage should explain."

"Sure, yeah." I suddenly feel itchy all over, as if invisible insects have swarmed me. But I know that's just nerves. "First off, I want you to know that I never blamed you for anything, and I never had any animosity toward you."

"Why would you? I never did anything. You're the one who walked out."

"But had started arguing a lot. Both of us bear some responsibility for that, though I know I was mostly to blame."

She puckers her lips, her gaze nailed to mine. Then she blows out a breath. "No, it wasn't mostly you. We both participated in the arguments, and I didn't do enough to calm things down."

"I think we just didn't know how to handle not having our kids around anymore."

"Are you offering the empty-nest defense?"

"Yes."

She crosses her legs and gazes out at the ocean. "Maybe we did suffer from that. But we also simply lost interest in each other. Can you remember the last time we had sex? Before we came here, I mean."

"No, I can't remember. That's pathetic, isn't it?"

Vanessa turns halfway toward me, laying her arm across the bench's back. "We both started working out more and got in better shape. But it doesn't seem like we did that to attract lovers. Of course, I have no idea what your love life has been like. Mine has been...depressingly dull."

Though I worry her answer might wreck me, I feel like I need to ask. "Have you, uh, slept with other men?"

She averts her gaze, but only for a moment. Then she looks at me, though she swallows hard enough I can see the movement in her throat. "I slept with two men, but those experiences were disappointing. I only dated three men. What about you?"

"I had sex with one woman, but we both realized immediately afterward that we'd made a mistake. I dated five women, but nothing ever worked out." I turn toward her, resting my elbow on the bench's back. "Why do you think we could never make it work with anybody else?"

"You want it to mean that we belong together."

"I want to know what you think."

She taps one finger on the bench. "Before I tell you that, I need to know why you divorced me. The real reason, not the vague bullshit you gave me at the time."

What I need to tell her will sound stupid, but I can't help that. If she accepts my reasoning for the divorce, then maybe I'll tell her about the trick I played to get her on this island. No, I can't ever tell her that. But keeping the secret would make me the world's biggest jackass.

I take a deep breath and just do it. "The truth is—"

Vanessa's phone chimes, indicating a new text. She fumbles with getting the phone out of the little purse she has draped diagonally across her body. Once she manages to bring out her phone, she makes a sheepish face. "Sorry. I forgot I signed up for a shopping trip to Suva. That's in Fiji."

Maybe this is a cosmic sign that it's too early for me to tell her everything. Or maybe I'm just a coward who's relieved I've been given a reprieve.

But then I get a great idea. "Could I come along on that trip? Or is it for the ladies only?"

"Anyone can go." She eyes me with suspicion. "Why do you want to join a shopping trip? You hate that kind of thing."

Time for a bit of honesty, even if it's embarrassing. "I'd like to spend time with you, even if we aren't getting back together. We started out as friends. Can't we try to get back to that? I miss talking to you, Nessa."

She glances at her phone, then sighs. "It is a group shopping excursion. And I'd like us to be friends again too, so you might as well come along."

Not exactly an enthusiastic invitation, but I'll take it.

Chapter Eleven

Vanessa

Our trip to Suva begins with a hike to the grass airstrip where all guests land when they first come to the island. The resort has two planes, one four-seater and another that can accommodate a dozen passengers plus the pilot, Rene Walker. He's quite a character, and he reminds me of Crocodile Dundee, though not only because he's Australian. He has that same devil-may-care attitude and sense of humor. But Rene doesn't wear the Crocodile Dundee outfit. Instead, he dresses like a beach bum.

Emilio has come along to be our tour guide and keep us from wandering off and getting lost.

Craig and I wind up sitting in the two seats closest to the cockpit, though a narrow aisle separates us. We're close enough to chat, but the couple in front of us insists on being friendly, and they are a genuinely nice, cheerful pair. I can tell Craig is disappointed that he doesn't have me all to himself, though he doesn't let it show enough that anyone else would notice.

I can't deny that I'm slightly relieved by this development. It gives me a reprieve from discussing our shared past.

The hour-long flight goes by quickly thanks to our new friends, Dale and Marcy Hicks. They're older than Craig and I are, and they're also the only senior-citizen couple on Heirani Motu. I never would have imagined that seniors would want to visit a nudist resort. Of course, we all had to wear clothes for our trip to Suva. Craig stunned me by wearing a Hawaiian shirt and khaki shorts. I've never seen him dressed that way before, not even when we actually went to Hawaii. He doesn't like shorts.

Yet he's wearing them. And he has no problem going nude.

I guess I don't know him as well as I thought.

As soon as we've landed on Suva, at the international airport, Rene pokes his head out of the cockpit and grins. "We're here, mates! Don't forget your bathers and watch out for the mozzies. You didn't even need to chuck a sickie to go on this trip."

I lean toward him and whisper, "Aren't you laying on the Aussie slang a bit thick, Rene?"

He winks. "Yeah, but the tourists love it."

"What did all of that mean, anyway?"

"I told everyone to remember their bathing suits and watch out for the mosquitoes. 'Chuck a sickie' means to call in sick for work when you aren't sick at all."

"Oh, I get it. I may need to use that term when I go back to work."

He gives me a devilish smile, then hollers to everyone, "Your rellies will be jealous you got to see Fiji. But watch out for the surfies when you're on the beach."

"Translation?" I whisper.

"Rellies are relatives, and surfies are people who surf."

"Gotcha. I'll have lots of new words to confuse my students with when I get home."

"If ya need more Aussie slang, just ask."

Craig and I wait while the other passengers disembark, then we follow Dale and Marcy down the aisle. Though I had landed on Suva just two days ago, I didn't really get to see the island. I'd jumped off a commercial airliner and hopped straight onto the resort's jet. Now, I get the chance to take in the surroundings. The airport isn't especially beautiful, but then, airports rarely are. A bus is waiting to ferry us around the city of Suva, and it's not an ordinary bus. As we march over there and climb inside, I realize our hosts have provided luxury transportation.

We visit all sorts of shops and eventually end up inside a quirky establishment that sells all kinds of knickknacks and novelties. I buy a cute little pair of cowrie shell earrings. But my ex-husband disapproves.

"Come on, Vanessa, those only cost ten bucks. Buy something extravagant. This is a vacation, after all."

"Therefore I should blow lots of money?"

"Exactly."

I shake my head and head over to a display of handwoven purses. Craig wanders away, out of my sight. Well, at least he can't tempt me to buy something extravagant if he's elsewhere. Craig used to be a diehard penny pincher. Now, he wants me to splurge. I guess I don't know him as well as I thought. But I can't deny I like this side of him. His new devil-may-care attitude is kind of sexy.

Maybe that explains why I let him screw me on the beach.

Once our shopping excursion ends, we head to a restaurant for lunch. Then we ride the luxury bus back to the airport. The driver is Emilio, and he parks thirty feet away from the jet so we don't need to walk very far. I'm impressed by all the perks the resort offers. They must have wealthy investors to pay for all of it.

An hour later, we're back on Heirani Motu.

We all traipse back to the resort, and the various couples split off to do their own thing. That leaves me and Craig with Emilio. He walks with us back to the lobby, but then, of course, he needs to go back to work. We might be on vacation, but Emilio is an employee.

In the lobby, Craig and I just stand here like we have no idea what to do next. I certainly have no clue how to politely say goodbye. It should be easy. *Have a good afternoon, Craig, see you around the resort.* But I can't speak the words. Instead, I swing my arms and hunch my shoulders. Craig scratches the back of his head and scrunches up his face.

Then he clears his throat. "So, ah, are you going to the masquerade party?"

"Um, I guess so. Might as well see what body paint is all about."

"Edible body paint."

I laugh, but it sounds nervous even to my ears. What, am I suddenly a sorority girl? No, I'm a mature woman who should not get embarrassed by edible body paint. I can show my students how to dissect a frog without flinching. This bizarre masquerade party won't faze me at all.

"What kind of costume will you paint onto your body?" I ask. "There will probably be a lot of superheroes, don't you think?"

"Emilio said they hired a professional body paint artist. I'm sure that person can come up with something more interesting than Batman."

I go back to swinging my arms while he goes back to scratching his head. One of us has to end this verbal torture, so I guess it might as well be me. I pat his arm, though I can't figure out why. "Have a good afternoon, Craig, see you at the party."

Before he can respond, I hustle down the hallway to my suite.

As I reach for the doorknob, I realize someone has taped a sealed envelope on the door at eye level. It has my name scrawled on it in beautiful calligraphy. I tear the envelope away from the door and go inside, while my curiosity grows with every passing second. I hurry over to the bed and sit on its edge as I tear the envelop open and pull out the ivory-colored card.

Vanessa, you are invited to our inaugural body-paint masquerade party. Our artist will create a costume specially for you, so please stop by Room 128 at seven forty-five pm. We hope you will enjoy this unique event. The note is signed "The Au Naturel Staff."

I can't deny I'm getting excited about this party.

On the back of the note, instructions have been written. I'm supposed to shower before six o'clock and not apply any lotions, powders, perfumes or similar things that might make applying the paint more difficult. Surely this party won't be too wild. It might be a nudist resort, but this isn't a den of debauchery.

I hang out on my private patio, under the shade of the palm tree hut, and let the sounds of the ocean lull me into a half-asleep state. I'd set the alarm on my nightstand to wake me up by five o'clock in case I fall asleep. I don't expect that to happen, and I don't realize I've drifted off until the alarm blares. Time to go to the dining hall for a little snack, then shower in preparation for the big party.

Now, the moment has arrived. Am I really going to let a stranger spray-paint my body? Well, why the hell not? I brush my teeth and my hair, then check the resort map in my welcome packet to find out where Room 128 is located.

A few minutes later, I knock on the door.

It swings open, and Holly Bythesea grins at me. "I'm so glad you're here, Vanessa. The party will be so much fun."

She's already "dressed" for the masquerade. She seems to have chosen a costume reminiscent of a blue fairy, complete with delicate wings that fold around her torso and cover breasts. Well, not actually. The artist who painted her up has done an incredible job, so good in fact that I can hardly believe it isn't a real costume.

"Wow, Holly, you look amazing. Do we pick our own costumes? Or does the artist choose?"

"It's a collaboration." She twirls around. "Do you really like it?"

"Yes. I can't wait to get my costume done."

Holly sidles past me, and as she leaves, she whispers, "Remember, the paint is edible."

Why do people keep reminding me of that fact? It's bizarre.

I shuffle into Room 128, half expecting to meet a goth person who has a stainless steel nose ring and lip piercings, not to mention black leather clothing and pink, spiked hair. But no, the woman who stands at a small table, fussing with a spray-paint gun dresses like a normal person.

When she notices me, she smiles and offers me her hand. "You must be Vanessa. I'm Lucy. I can't wait to work with you on finding the perfect painted costume. You have a lovely figure, so it won't be hard at all to make you look incredible."

"Thank you. I'm looking forward to this. I've never had any kind of body-paint costume before."

"Would you mind spinning around for me, slowly? I'd like to get the full picture before we talk about costumes."

"Sure." I turn in a circle while she studies me like I'm an abstract painting in a museum. "That's enough. Let's spitball ideas."

I stand where Lucy tells me to and follow her instructions about when to lift this arm and when to lift that arm. She focuses on her work intently as she creates a sort of trompe l'oeil effect on my skin so that my bare feet seem to be covered by boots. Once she finishes painting my body, Lucy adds the final touches—streaks in my hair and a few props. When I look at myself in a full-length mirror, I can't believe what I see. This body-paint costume would probably fool anybody on the street. It looks that real.

Yet I'm still abiding by the resort rules of no clothes.

As I take one last look at myself in the mirror, I need to ask a question. "How do I get this stuff off after the party?"

"You can wash it off in the shower," Lucy says. "Or you could let your partner lick it off. The paint is edible, after all."

"Oh, right," I say with a nervous laugh, because an image of Craig just flashed in my mind. No, he will not lick my body clean. It would be inappropriate. "I don't have a partner, so I'll be washing it off. Do I use regular bath soap?"

"Sure. Any kind you like."

I turn away from the mirror, facing Lucy. "You are an incredible artist. Thank you for making a middle-aged mom look so good."

"You look great without any body paint. I just gave you a little more pizzazz. Enjoy the party, Vanessa."

I walk out the door and return to my suite, per the resort's instructions for this event. At precisely eight-thirty, I make my way out to the main patio. A thrill ripples through me, though I can't imagine why. This is just a party. But that sensation refuses to go away. I step out onto the patio and glance around, taking in the sensual lighting and music, as well as the guests who are gradually arriving. Zach waves to me, in a strictly friendly way since he has a pretty girl tucked under his arm.

Then I see Craig, and my jaw drops.

Chapter Twelve

Craig

As I walk out onto the patio, I catch sight of Vanessa standing alone on the far side, near where the woods begin and the trail leads off into the wilds. She seems rather uncomfortable, like she's waiting for someone to tell her where to go and what to do. But I barely notice all of that. My focus has become glued to her body and the costume painted onto her shapely figure. She's always beautiful, but now...I can hardly breathe while I drink in the vision of her. The younger women in the crowd can't hold a candle to Vanessa.

She's dressed like some sort of ancient Greek fantasy character, a goddess or a witch or who knows what. I don't care what her costume portrays. My focus has telescoped down to her body and nothing else. As I wend my way through the crowd, she seems unaware that I'm coming toward her, too busy scanning the patio for something or someone.

Whether she knows it or not, she's searching for me.

Vanessa startles when I halt in front of her. "Oh. I didn't see you coming."

"I know. What were you looking for?"

"Nothing, really. I think I'm having trouble getting used to the idea of a painted-on costume."

I rake my gaze over her, starting with her hair that's been fluffed up and has purple streaks in it. I would never have thought I'd like that, but I do. Her hair goes with her pseudo-outfit. I'd met

Lucy, the body paint expert, earlier this evening when she sprayed on my costume, and I learned just how meticulous she is about making body paint look realistic. As I absorb the details of Vanessa's costume, though, I find it hard to concentrate on the artistry. All I can think about is how hot she looks.

Her breasts hang normally, but the way Lucy shaded the undersides makes it seem like they're being held up by a bra. The painted on garment looks like a cobalt-blue halter top with gold straps that crisscross her chest. She has fake tattoos splashed across her torso diagonally and more that wind around one leg. The tattoos remind me of patterns on ancient Greek pottery. The illusion of shorts covers her groin and upper thighs, similar to the way Wonder Woman's outfit looks, but without the stars-and-stripes motif.

For a moment, I stare at the necklace that drapes over her shoulders because I swear it's real. Then Vanessa shifts her feet a touch, and I realize the jewelry is an illusion too. That includes gold bracelets on her wrists. She seems to be wearing boots, but I quickly deduce that those are also illusions. Vanessa isn't just painted up like a Greek priestess. She is a genuine sex goddess.

My cock jerks, but I don't think she noticed that.

Vanessa skims her gaze over my body—and licks her lips, though that must be an unconscious gesture. "What are you supposed to be?"

I love that her voice has grown huskier. "Lucy told me I'm Hercules meets Conan the Barbarian."

"Whatever your costume is, I like it." She gives me another once over and licks her lips again. "I take that back. I don't like it, I love it."

That doesn't mean she loves *me*, but I'll take what I can get. Damn, I need to make love to her, need it so fiercely that I can barely breathe. I want to lay her down on the soft grass and lick all that body paint off her skin.

She loves my costume because Lucy painted me up to look like an outrageously buff barbarian, complete with a faux loincloth. I have no clue how she accomplished that illusion. Lucy is a genius. She also shaded my body so that it seems like I have bigger muscles than I actually do.

I clasp Vanessa's hand, and she doesn't pull away. So, I push for a little more. "Want to go to your suite and sit on the patio?"

"We just got here. Wouldn't it be rude to sneak away right after the party started?"

"Do you care?" I move closer, still holding her hand, threading my fingers with hers. Then I lower my head until my lips brush the shell of her ear. "I want you, Vanessa, even more than I did on the beach. You are the most beautiful, sensual woman on earth, and I need to lick that costume off your skin."

"The beach was a one-time thing. We agreed to that."

"No, you told me that's what it was. I never agreed to anything." I flick my tongue out to tease her lobe. "The way you looked at me when you first saw me, it proved that you want me to fuck you."

Her breasts are rising and falling more heavily. "We shouldn't. I don't want you to get the wrong idea about us."

The wrong idea? I love her. There's nothing wrong about that. I can't show her how I feel while we're surrounded by people, which means I need to convince her to go with me to her suite. And I know exactly how to do that.

I pull her earlobe into my mouth, coiling my tongue around it over and over until she sucks in a sharp breath. Her nipples have hardened. I slide my hand into her hair to tip her head back. Then I drag my tongue up the column of her throat, flicking it to arouse her even more, and wait for the sign.

She sighs, and her posture relaxes.

Bingo. I claim her mouth and slide my tongue between her lips. Rather than pulling away, she grasps my biceps and teases my tongue the way I'm teasing hers. She releases the sweetest, most erotic little grunt.

I peel my lips away from hers. "Your suite?"

"Yes, please, now."

Still holding her hand, I lead her across the patio and through the lobby, straight down the corridor where her suite lies. She fumbles to unlock the door with her keycard, which she had retrieved from the front desk, finally managing the task on the third try. We hurry into her room, but when she starts to head for the bed, I grab her arm and pull her back to me, caging her against the door. Then I press my body to hers.

"Here?" she whispers. "The bed—"

"Right here, Nessa."

I take hold of her hands, raising them until I can cuff her wrists to the door just above her head. While her breathing grows ragged, I bow my head to scrape my tongue over the painted strap on her shoulder. "Mm, tastes like raspberry. But nothing tastes as good as your cream." I take another lick, dragging my tongue slowly down the faux strap. "I won't lick all the paint off you. I plan to find all your sweet spots and tease you with my tongue until you're panting for me. But that's just the beginning of what I want to do with you."

I bend my knees to level my face with her tit and scrape my tongue around that peak in a circular motion that makes her moan.

"Please, Craig, take me now."

"Not yet."

She kicks my shin. "Yes, now, dammit."

A chuckle rumbles out of me, and since I have my mouth on her nipple, my lips vibrate against her skin. She gasps and arches her back.

"Unh, please, Craig."

"Fuck, I love it when you beg." I release her wrists. "Keep your hands up, Nessa. That's an order. Disobey me and I'll spank you."

Her eyes widen—but with lustful surprise, not disgust. I have never in my life spanked a woman, but I suddenly want to do all kinds of naughty things with her. Maybe this is some kind of strange midlife crisis, but I don't care. Making love to Vanessa is all I can focus on right now.

I lower myself inch by inch with my hands ghosting along her sides. I pause at her navel, where Lucy had created the illusion of a belly-button ring with a glistening ruby at its center. The first flick of my tongue makes Vanessa jerk and arch her back again. But when I begin to swirl my tongue round and round in her navel, lapping up the raspberry-flavored paint, she rocks her hips as if she's begging me to fuck her with my mouth.

Not yet. I love making her squirm and moan.

She spreads her thighs.

My mouth waters at the scent of her cream, but I won't lose track of my strategy. Drive Vanessa crazy, that's my plan. Make her want me so badly she'll take me back.

I slide my tongue lightly down her belly while she squirms more, and when I reach her mound, I realize the body paint is covering the hairs there. I assumed Lucy had shaved Vanessa. But no, she simply painted over the hairs. I trace my tongue over the skin just above her mound, rewarded by her soft gasp and the hungry noise she makes, somewhere between a moan and a whimper.

Her every response gets me harder and hotter for her.

While she claws the door with her fingernails, I lick her inner thigh, cleaning off the paint and simultaneously getting her even more turned on. I move to the other thigh, laving it with my tongue. My hair grazes her skin and tickles it, I'm sure, based on the way her tits are heaving and she scrapes the door faster, almost frantically.

"Turn around," I command. "Show me your ass, Nessa."

She flips around and splays her palms on the door, her cheek plastered to its surface while she gazes down at me. I palm her ass cheeks and give each a light squeeze, just enough to make her bite down on her lip so hard it turns white.

I kiss one cheek, then lick the paint off with quick swipes before I lick my way up her spine, moving swiftly, keeping the touch light. When I get to her neck, I push her hair away and drag my lips over the bare flesh there.

She wriggles and grunts. "Enough with the foreplay. I want you inside me now."

"Anything for you, Nessa." I pick her up. "But first, we need to clean off all this body paint."

"But I want to lick it off you. It's only fair."

"Your sheets might get covered in paint."

She laughs. "Since when do you care about sheets getting dirty? I don't recall you ever volunteering to wash them."

"Fair point." I start walking toward the bathroom. "Tell you what, I'll let you taste my body paint before we wash each other off."

Taste my body paint. Now there's a phrase I never imagined I would have spoken. I think this island has magical brainwashing capabilities because I've done things here that I would've laughed at if anyone back home had suggested them. The bathroom has no door, but I shouldn't be surprised by that fact. This is a wicked naturist resort. My little bungalow does have a door, though. I guess they think the peons are privacy nuts.

I set Vanessa down in front of the double sinks and a big mirror in the bathroom. The huge shower stall seems big enough to hold an entire baseball team, and it has enough heads to create a downpour. I'm glad Vanessa has the top-notch suite. She deserves it after the way I dumped her three years ago.

She leans back against the counter, hands on the edge, tapping one finger as she studies me.

I take a step toward her, but she pushes me away with one foot. "Uh-uh-uh. Let me consider the options before I put my tongue on you."

"Take all the time you want, baby."

"You never called me 'baby' when we were together."

I shrug. "Times change. People change too."

And I need her to accept that or I'll never win her back.

She pushes away from the counter, now standing inches away, and traces her tongue over her lips, top and bottom, while scrutinizing me some more. Then she smirks and sinks down toward the floor. Her body undulates like a cobra coiling itself into its basket again. But when her face reaches my groin, she drops to her knees and leans forward.

And she drags her tongue up the length of my erection.

I suck in a breath.

She blows a stream of warm air over my crown, smirking again when I flinch. "I love how your dick is painted to look like a rope, and it's part of the fake rope that encircles your hips."

"I thought it was strange at first, but Lucy convinced me a golden rope would be 'awesome.' "

"She was right." Vanessa tips her head back to look at me. "And now I'm going to wipe all that paint off your dick with my tongue."

Chapter Thirteen

Vanessa

I'm staring at Craig's dick from a few inches away, and I'm about to clean off his skin with my tongue. This isn't something middle-aged people do, is it? When my parents got into their fifties, they started playing golf on the weekends. When they both retired, they moved to Florida to live in one of those communities for seniors. I am the same age my mom was when she bought her first golfing outfit.

But I'm not teeing up on the green. No, I'm about to swallow my ex-husband's cock and lick the edible paint off his body.

I've never wanted to do anything more than I want this.

My first taste of him was strawberry flavored, thanks to the paint. Now, I set my hands on his thighs and lean in to lap up every speck of the edible paint until I've cleaned off almost all of his cock. Then I grasp the base.

He pushes a hand into my hair.

When I gaze up at him, the hunger on his face takes my breath away. He never wanted me this much before. I'll consider the question of why later on. Right now, I need to taste him, not the paint. He groans when I swipe my tongue over the head of his erection, licking away the bead of moisture there. Mm, now that's the flavor I want to devour.

He watches my every move, our gazes locked, and massages my scalp with his fingertips.

I take him into my mouth, licking and sucking, teasing his crown. The natural flavor of him arouses me more than any edible paint could. His breathing grows heavier. I pump his length while lavishing it with my tongue. He groans deeply, letting his head fall back. I grasp his sac and massage it, making him gasp, then slide my fingers under his dick to rub the perineum.

"Fuck," he snarls. "Vanessa—Ah, you're killing me."

In the best way, I'm sure, though I can't say so. I've still got his dick in my mouth, and I have no intention of pulling away yet. So, I coil my tongue round and round his length while rubbing that sweet spot. Just when I'm sure he's on the edge of climax, based on the way his face is cinched up tight, I pull away.

And I rise just as slowly as I'd lowered myself. "Let's get clean, Craig. Then we can get dirty again in bed."

He glances down at his dick. "Uh, do we need condoms?"

"No. I'm post-menopausal, remember? And I had a hysterectomy. You can't get me pregnant. If you're worried I might have STDs..."

"Of course not. You've only been with two men since our divorce, right? That's what you said. It's the same for me, and I used protection both times."

"Same for me. That means we can screw each other au naturel, which seems appropriate since we're naked all the time on this island."

He grins. "I love the way your scientist mind works, but I never imagined you'd use it to justify fucking in the shower without a condom."

"Maybe sometime I'll talk dirty to you in biology jargon."

"I'd love that."

Craig turns on the shower and gets the temperature just right, then picks me up and carries me into the stall. He pulls the door shut, and steam begins to rise around us.

I'm standing under one of the five showerheads, leaning against the wall. "I'm liking your new obsession with carrying me. It's surprisingly sexy."

"Glad you approve. We've both changed over the years, but coming to this island has been a revelation."

"Yes, it has." I gently kick his shin. "Now, are you going to fuck me anytime soon? Or should I order a late-night snack to be delivered to the bathroom?"

"I might need to punish you for being so sarcastic."

"Go on. I dare you."

He plants his hands on the shower wall at either side of my head, then bends his elbows until our faces hover millimeters apart. "Right now, all I want to do is make you feel good."

"I'm on board for that." My voice has changed, dropping to a lower, sultrier register. I can't help it. He's turning me on in ways he has never done before, and I love it.

Craig brushes his lips over mine so delicately, while his breaths tease my skin. That simple act arouses me even more, so much that I suck in a shaky breath and my clit pulses. He sweeps his mouth over mine, back and forth, twice. My pulse beats hard enough that I can hear it throbbing. But when he flicks his tongue out and darts it between my lips, I let out a sharp, whimpering cry. Holy shit, was that me making that desperate sound? I've never done that before.

He stares directly into my eyes. "I want to rub my dick up and down your folds until you're writhing and begging me to make you come."

"I don't get as wet as I used to. Need lube to—"

"Not this time. I remember how wet you were on the beach yesterday." He lays a hand on my belly, holding it there for just long enough that a sultry tingle sweeps over my skin. Then he drags that hand down ever so slowly until his fingers brush my mound. He hesitates again, and my pulse revs up even more. But when he slides one finger between my folds, I know he's right. I won't need lube this time. Somehow, he has gotten me so aroused that I feel like a teenager again.

He pushes my thighs apart with one hand, then shoves it between my legs to cup my sex. "I'll take you to the edge and keep you balanced there until I'm ready for you to come."

Craig was definitely never like this before. But I love it.

And I can't believe the words I speak now. "Do anything you want to me. Fuck me with your hand as long as you fuck me with your dick too."

He growls. I swear he does that. My husband had never behaved this way, but my ex has turned into a sex god. Who knew?

Craig rubs my cleft in slow strokes, gazing into my eyes the entire time, gradually increasing the pace in a way that's sure to drive me insane. I'm struggling to catch my breath. My body is on fire in the best way. But when he kisses me, I lose control so completely that I can't think anymore. All I can do is feel. He shifts his hand so he can rub my cleft with his fingers and my clit with the heel of his hand, and soon, I'm teetering on the edge.

A desperate cry bursts out of me.

He pushes my thighs further apart with one knee. While his kisses turn hotter and deeper, he thrusts into me and holds that position until I'm whimpering, my cries dampened by his mouth on mine. Just when I think I'll have a heart attack any second, he begins to pump in and out at a measured pace. He coils his tongue around mine, over and over, in time with his thrusts. My wetness creates a sucking sound. He grunts and takes me harder, faster, making my body bounce and scrape across the smooth wall of the shower.

The tension builds inside me, like a live wire being stretched taut, the sparks igniting a fire within my body, within my sex.

"Come for me, Nessa. Come for me now."

I wrap my legs around his hips and my arms around his neck, crushing him to my body. He grunts and groans, punching into me with so much power that I can't hold back any longer. I sink my nails into his back as the orgasm explodes inside me. A half-strangled scream erupts out of me while my inner muscles grip his cock again and again, and finally, he blows apart inside me with a shout that echoes through the bathroom.

For a moment after it's all over, we don't move a single muscle. I'm still wrapped around him. My head had fallen onto his shoulder in the instant after the climax ended, and I can't manage to lift it yet. His dick is still nestled within my body.

At last, I find the strength to lift my head and look into his eyes. "That was...unexpected."

He tries to chuckle but doesn't have enough breath for that yet. "Yeah, that was a surprise for sure."

"Your dirty talk was fantastic. Why didn't you ever talk that way when we made love while we were married?"

"Don't know. Sometimes I wanted to, but I never did."

Without thinking about what I'm doing, I begin to comb my fingers through his wet hair. "I'm glad you finally did it. This is a new side of you that I love seeing."

"Do you want to see it again?"

"Yes." I answered his question without even pausing to consider the ramifications. Of course I want more mind-blowing sex with Craig. That doesn't mean we're getting back together. This is a vacation fling, right? Or maybe that's just what I'm convincing myself to believe. "Let's go into the bedroom and try screwing each other in a different way."

"Not sure I can come up with something else right now. Pretty sure my brain has melted."

"Mine too." I chew on my lip for a moment, then give up and tell the truth, no matter how embarrassing it might be. "I don't want this to end yet. Let's order a snack from room service and then come up with another way to fuck."

"Sounds perfect."

Craig finds a large sponge on a little shelf and uses that to clean off the paint that remains on my skin. Then I do the same for him. This is another first for us. In our more than three decades of marriage, we had never showered together and certainly never had sex in the shower. Maybe we have both changed. Is that a bad thing? Or a good thing? It's too soon to know.

But a part of me I've been suppressing wants it to be a good thing. I can't stand another heartbreak, though. He threw me away once, and who's to say he won't do it again.

After drying off with a couple of big, plush towels, we return to the bedroom and lie down on the equally plush mattress with the covers pulled back. I've never slept on a bed this comfortable in all my life. The resort really does go all out for their guests. I grab the room service menu from the nightstand drawer and start to browse the menu. But soon, I hear soft snoring emanating from the other side of the bed.

I glance at Craig.

He's asleep, naturally. I should have guessed he would nod off since that was often what happened after we made love back when we were married. We're both older now, so that would make us both more likely to pass out after sex, especially when we fucked like the horniest teenagers on earth. I loved every minute of this night, so I won't complain. But as I watch him sleeping, I get a pang in my chest that I haven't experienced in a long time.

No, I can't be falling for him all over again. I won't risk another heartbreak.

I set the menu on the nightstand and pull the covers over us, crawling under the sheets to lie beside him. No cuddling. I might be experiencing a strange kind of sentimental reaction to our hot time in the bathroom, but I refuse to let him wheedle his way back into my heart so easily. I need to remain circumspect. This was great sex, nothing more. Just a casual fling.

The workout we both got this evening has left me wiped out, though in a good way. I drift off to sleep without even realizing it. When I wake up, the sun is already shining through the patio doors and the full-length windows alongside them. For a moment, I just lie here gazing out at the deep blue sky and the smattering of puffy little clouds that lazily ride the currents high above. The scent of flowers wafts in through the open patio doors. I stretch and sigh, feeling more contented than I have in years.

A sharp snort yanks me out of my reverie.

When I glance at the man beside me, who had produced that snort, he still has his eyes shut and a faint smile on his lips.

I veer my gaze to the ceiling. No, I will not fall for him again. Never.

<h1 style="text-align:center">Chapter Fourteen</h1>

Craig

I had the best dream last night, one that involved Vanessa, yet even that dream can't compare to what we did last night. Though I've woken up, I still haven't managed to open my eyes. Memories of last night keep replaying in my mind. The masquerade party had led to the best night of my life, all because Vanessa admitted she wanted to have sex with me. She insisted it wouldn't mean anything, just a fling, but I will never believe that's what she wants.

My ex-wife went down on me. She licked paint off my body. That has to mean something more than a quick way to get off. It's possible I'm a pigheaded moron, but I can't accept that the woman I've known for nearly four decades doesn't have any feelings for me at all. Not after last night.

A throat-clearing yanks me out of my trance.

I open one eye and smile when I see Vanessa lying beside me. Then I open the other eye and finally notice her demeanor. Lips crimped. Hands tightly clasped over her belly. Gaze aimed at the ceiling. I can see one toe tapping beneath the covers too.

"What's wrong?" I ask. "You seem annoyed. Incredible sex is supposed to be relaxing."

"You shouldn't have spent the night."

I yawn and stretch, sighing with more contentment that I've ever felt before. "Come on, Vanessa. You can admit that last night was great. It won't cause the world to tilt off its axis."

She moans and covers her face with her hands. Then she mumbles something I can't understand.

Rolling onto my side, I prop myself up with one elbow and gently peel her fingers away from her eyes. "Tell me why you're panicking."

"Not panicking." She sighs, and her whole body goes limp. "This was supposed to be a one-night stand."

"Who said that? Not me."

"I said it. And I meant it, Craig." She sits up and swings her legs over the side of the bed, giving me her back. "Please go. Our fling is over, so there's no reason for you to stay here in my suite."

"Okay, if that's what you want." I don't want that, and I'm sure she doesn't really want it either. I've known her for too long to believe that. But I should give her time to come to terms with it.

I have less than two weeks to convince her.

Though I head for the dining hall, I don't feel particularly hungry. That's probably because Vanessa kicked me to the curb again. I had known from the start, since the day I came up with my deceitful plan, that winning her heart again would be the most difficult task I've ever undertaken. Should I tell her what I did to get her on this island? Deceit is rarely a good thing, but I did all of this for her. She wouldn't talk to me before we came here. Sure, she was polite during the few times when we saw each other after the divorce. But I don't want polite, awkward conversation. I want my wife.

How will she feel if she finds out about my deception?

I can't worry about that right now. Whether she'll hate me or not is a moot point unless I can make some headway with rekindling what we used to have. No, that's not right. I don't want what we used to have. I want something better, stronger, deeper. We had a good marriage, but those days are gone. We need to develop a mature relationship that's not predicated on our kids being around as a buffer.

That thought makes me stop in the middle of chewing a cube of papaya. Is that what I thought our kids were? A buffer? Not sure why I had that thought. I love our Greg, Nicole, and April, and Vanessa loves them too. They aren't a tool for avoiding our relationship issues. I need to discuss all of this with Vanessa, if she'll let me.

How long should I wait before broaching the subject again?

I finish my breakfast while pondering that question, but I don't see Vanessa during that time. Either she prefers to eat later in the morning or she doesn't want to bump into me. I have no reasonable excuse for hanging around in the dining hall once I've finished eating, so I make my way out onto the big patio. I'm the only person sitting alone at a table. Couples enjoy breakfast outdoors at a smattering of other tables.

This resort really is for couples. I feel like a third wheel just sitting here, waiting for someone to beg me to hang out with them. At least I brought a magazine and a glass of lemonade. That makes me seem slightly less pathetic.

Zach ambles out onto the patio with a pretty young woman. They hold hands as they cross the space, having emerged from the side of the building rather than the lobby. Great, that's exactly who I want to see right now. The kid who tried to seduce my ex-wife. I hold my magazine up a little higher, trying to shield my face in the hope Zach won't notice me.

"Hey, Craig. Isn't this an awesome morning?"

Aw, shit. I must have miscalculated how high I needed to hold my magazine to use it as a shield. I lower the magazine and try to smile, though it comes out feeling rather forced. "Good morning, Zach."

"Mind if we join you?"

I don't want to seem like a jealous jerk, which means I have only one option. I smile again, this time doing my damnedest to seem happy. "Sure, I'd love some company."

Zach sits down opposite me, and his girlfriend takes the seat between us. "Oh, hey, I should introduce you. Craig Hathaway, meet Aspen Patel."

I smile at the girl. "It's nice to meet you, Aspen."

What kind of a name is that? An aspen is a tree, not a person. I will never understand the names younger generations choose for their children. But she seems like a sweet girl, and it's not her fault if her parents were drunk when they picked a name for her.

Fortunately, Zach and Aspen do most of the talking. I mainly have to sit here listening and pretending to care about whether that bird they saw yesterday was a cockatoo or a parrot. I might enjoy the conversation, sort of, if I weren't constantly thinking about Vanessa and last night. At least Zach has the good sense not to mention my ex-wife.

Until he does.

Zach grins at me. "Hey, I saw you and Vanessa heading down the woods trail yesterday. You guys must be getting along a lot better now." He gives me an exaggerated wink. "Might be wedding bells real soon, huh?"

"Don't spread that rumor. Vanessa likes to keep things private, so I can't confirm or deny what you implied."

He laughs. "I love the way you talk, man. It's like you're a secret agent or something."

Aspen leans forward, aiming her excited expression at me. "Are you really a secret agent?"

"Sorry, no. I'm a data scientist."

"Isn't that, like, kind of the same thing?"

"Not really."

She bites her bottom lip, and her brows wrinkle. "What is a data scientist?"

"I collate and analyze data to come up with stats and write reports so that businesses can better serve their customers."

"Wow, that sounds hard."

"I've been doing this job for fifteen years. It's old hat for me."

She touches my hand. "You should get a different hat. Something that would fit you better."

The girl I'd taken for a ditz just created a metaphor. A nice one. I need to stop judging younger people based on their behavior, and instead, find out if they have brains. Aspen seems to have that.

"Maybe you're right," I tell her. "My job has become a bit boring."

Aspen pokes her boyfriend's arm. "You should take that advice too, Zach. You told me you're sick of working at a call center, pestering people to buy insurance."

Zach sells insurance? All my preconceptions just got launched into outer space. Here on earth, reality is nothing like what I assumed.

"Aspen is right," I tell Zach. "If you hate your job, start looking for something different."

"I'll do it if you will."

"You're on."

Aspen claps her hands, but it's the kind of clapping people do during golf games. "Yay. I'm glad you guys are going to search for your dream jobs."

I can't help asking her a question. "What do you do for a living, Aspen?"

"Neuroscience. I'm working on my PhD."

Did I just do a double take, like a cartoon character? I think I did. Aspen really is not the ditz I thought she was.

Now that all my preconceptions have been blown apart by a nuclear bomb of reality, I have a nice conversation with Zach and Aspen. They seem perfect for each other, and they definitely have chemistry between them. As I watch the two of them, I can't help comparing their budding relationship with what Vanessa and I had for decades. Chemistry? For sure. Shared interests? Yeah, we had that too. When did things change? Oddly enough, Aspen provided a clue that I had ignored for too long.

Our marriage changed when I got a new job—as a data scientist.

Could it really be that simple? Well, I doubt it's simple. A lot of other factors played into the dissolution of our marriage. But maybe I've finally stumbled onto the key that will unlock the truth.

Yeah, even an old guy like me can do metaphors.

After a while, Zach and Aspen decide to go to the waterfall to swim. He wants to climb the cliff and jump off into the pool. They invite me to go along, and I believe that's a sincere invite, but I decline. Jumping off a cliff doesn't appeal to me. And all I want to do is find Vanessa.

I say goodbye to Zach and Aspen, then wander into the lobby to ask the desk clerk if he saw my ex-wife. The nice young man tells me no, he hasn't seen her. I wander outside and go to the miniten court, but nobody is there. I guess it's too early for a match. On my way back to the big patio, I bump into Holly Bythesea.

"Have you seen Vanessa?" I ask. "I've been looking for her."

"She had breakfast by the pool this morning, then she mentioned heading for the waterfall."

"That's the place in the woods, right? The one with a trail that's kind of hidden."

"Exactly." Holly wags her brows at me. "It's a very romantic spot."

"Don't get your hopes up. I haven't had much luck with wooing Vanessa."

"But you love her. That means you will find a way to get through to her."

I'd love to believe that, and last night gave me a slender thread of hope, but I'm losing faith in my ability to do that. "Did James tell you what I did?"

Holly's brows draw together. "What do you mean?"

"I guess he didn't tell you." I rub my jaw while I consider whether I should confess to her. I appreciate that James kept my secret, but maybe Holly can offer some advice that her husband wouldn't have thought of, being a guy. "Well, you see, I sort of tricked Vanessa into coming here."

Her brows shoot up now. "Tricked her? Ooh, this is getting juicy."

She might be the strangest woman I've ever met.

But I push that thought aside and continue. "I sent her a letter saying that she'd won a free two-week stay at this resort. But I actually paid for it all."

"And you made sure to be here when she arrived."

"Yes. I'm a complete asshole, right?"

She tips her head to the side, studying me. "There is an asshole-ish quality to what you did, but that doesn't mean you'll lose Vanessa if you fess up. I forgave James after he tricked me in a similar way."

"Yeah, he told me about that." I scratch my arm because it suddenly feels itchy, though I'm pretty sure it's a phantom itch. "Could you give me a little advice? No, that's too much to ask."

Holly smiles and bumps my arm. "Don't be so pessimistic. Vanessa loves you. I can see it, James can see it, and I bet even Vanessa herself realizes it. But you hurt her in a big way, and it'll take time to heal those wounds. Don't give up, that's my advice."

I want to ask her another question, but it's too embarrassing to talk about it with a young, beautiful woman like Holly. Of course, she works at a nudist resort and started out as a guest here. So, she's probably not shy about intimate matters.

"You want some sexy advice, don't you?" she says. "No need to ask. I'll email you some info that I think will be very helpful."

"Uh, thanks. How did you know what I wanted to ask about?"

She taps her temple. "Not just a pretty face. And I have great intuition."

Holly smiles and waves goodbye as she walks away.

I'm getting sex advice from a twenty-something married woman, and I'm receiving that information via email.

Oh yeah, I feel a thousand years old right now.

Chapter Fifteen

Vanessa

How long have I been lying here on this chaise, alone? Not sure. I've had my eyes closed since about thirty seconds after I arrived at this hidden spot. I'm letting the tropical forest atmosphere and the sounds of exotic wildlife soak into my psyche. I need some serious relaxation after that intensely erotic evening with Craig and the strong feelings I've experienced since then.

I loved last night. Loved it so much. And that's damn confusing.

But sex with Craig doesn't change our relationship. Does it?

The sultry air feels like warm silk on my skin, and the sunlight that filters down through the trees toasts my flesh just enough to make me feel like I've melted into a puddle of caramel. The sensation arouses me, though only enough that my nipples tighten. Mm, I love this feeling.

A memory sifts through my mind, hazy at first, then sharpening into a vivid reminder of last night. Craig naked and aroused and covered with paint. Me licking that paint off his body, then taking his cock into my mouth. The sensual sound of the water running in the shower, pattering like a gentle rain. The moment when he pushed me against the wall and thrust into me.

I'm growing slick between my thighs.

Though I shouldn't do it, I can't resist indulging in that memory while I stroke my skin delicately, turning myself on even more.

"Shit. Sorry."

My eyes fly open, and I scowl at Craig. "What on earth are you doing? You scared the living daylights out of me."

Yes, my heart is pounding now, but not because of my fantasy. He sneaked up on me. And I had just slipped two fingers between my folds when he suddenly turned up.

Craig saunters over to the chaise beside mine and lies down on it. "I am sorry I scared you. That wasn't my intention."

I flap my hands at him in a shooing motion. "Go away. I'm trying to have a private moment of relaxation."

"You define 'relaxation' as 'masturbation'?"

"None of your business."

He stretches a hand out to trail his fingertips over my upper arm. "You're already turned on. Might as well make use of that."

"That's a terrible idea." The way he keeps trailing his fingers up and down is driving me crazy. It feels so good that I know I'll give in soon if I can't chase him away. "Please, Craig, I need some alone time."

"I disagree. What we both need is orgasms." He finally pulls his hand away, but only so he can stroke his cock with that hand. "I'm halfway to hard, and knowing you were about to masturbate will get me all the way there fast."

Saying no to him has become almost impossible since I arrived on this island. Every time he suggests we do something naughty, he speaks those words in a husky, sensual voice that erases all my memories of why I should tell him to stop. I loved what we did on the beach. But last night... Holy shit, that was the most incredible sexual experience of my life.

Now he wants to do it again. Here in the woods.

I'm getting wetter just thinking about that, and a sultry tingle has started up between my thighs.

He sits up and sets his feet on the ground, roving his gaze over my entire body. Just watching him do that makes me even more aroused. If Craig had behaved this way when we were married, I would never have let him divorce me. Oh, now that's a rational suggestion. Stay married for the hot sex. I think I've lost about fifty IQ points in the past few days.

Craig leans toward me. "Tell me you absolutely do not want to have sex with me, and I'll go away. Be honest with yourself and me."

If I lie, he'll realize that. Craig knows me better than anyone. He's leveraging that fact as part of seducing me. But I'm not a silly inge-nue. I'm a mature woman who can say no to any man, no matter how pushy he gets. Craig isn't pushy, though, and for some reason I can't say no to him anymore.

"You're conflicted, Vanessa. I can see it on your face. Why does this have to be such a big deal for you?"

"Because we're divorced, and you dumped me."

"I'm sorry. I should never have done that."

I sit up and face him. "Apologizing is all well and good, but I need explanations. You were going to give me that, or so you said. Then my phone rang, and we both forgot about finishing our discussion."

"Let's finish it now."

"Okay. Go on and tell me."

He squirms and makes an uncomfortable face. Then he sighs. "I love you, Vanessa. Always have, always will. But I could tell you were unhappy. You lost interest in me because I was working too damn hard. I hated my job and should've quit, to show you that the most important thing in my life is you, even without kids in the house."

"It's true that everything changed when the kids moved out. Once our youngest was gone, we had to learn how to talk to each other again. And we didn't do a good job of that."

"April leaving was part of the problem. But we had gotten into a rut before that, one that only deepened afterward." He clasps his hands and stares down at them. "You kept saying that we never had any fun, everything was stale and boring. You even lost interest in sex."

"I know. And I used to blame you for that, but it's not fair to lay it all on you. I missed my babies. They don't need me anymore, and I guess the empty-nest syndrome hit me hard."

"Yeah, me too. But I couldn't find a way to tell you that." He looks up at me, smiling ruefully. "I'm a typical man, the kind who's ashamed to admit that he doesn't know what the hell to do. My wife was miserable, and I could think of only one way to fix the problem."

"By dumping me."

"It's not quite that simple. I believed that setting you free was the only way to spare you from more pain." He shakes his head. "I'm a moron. I know that. Over the past three years, I've come to realize I made a horrible mistake. You are the only woman for me."

"And you think you're the only man for me."

"No. I hope I can win you back, but I know it will be a long, hard road to accomplish that."

"Yes, it will."

He stares at me for a moment without blinking. Then he swallows hard enough that the movement is visible in his throat. "Are you saying there's a chance I could win you back?"

I hadn't meant to give him that hope. But I don't want to completely shut down the idea either. Coming to Heirani Motu has affected me in ways that I can't fully articulate, and I'm starting to see things in a different light. Does that mean I want to reconcile with Craig? The question comes with so many caveats that I don't know how to respond. All I can do is be honest.

"That's not a yes or no question, Craig. We were married for a long time, then you threw our marriage away seemingly on a whim. I need time to think about what you've told me and what it might mean to our relationship."

"I get it, I do." He looks so dejected that I want to hug him, but that would only confuse things even more. "I'll wait forever for you, Vanessa. You're my soul mate."

Since when does he believe in soul mates? Craig used to scoff at that sort of thing, and so did I. He seems to have become a true romantic over the past three years.

I get up and give him the best smile I can, though it's a tight one. "I'll think about everything you said. That's the best I can offer."

He jumps up, his expression brightening. "Thank you, Nessa."

As I walk away from him, I fight the impulse to glance back. For reasons I can't explain, I feel like I've betrayed him by not immediately jumping into his arms and offering to marry him again. That's ridiculous. Even Craig doesn't expect me to do that. I don't know if two weeks on this island will change anything, but I'm about to find out one way or another.

The moment I enter the lobby, I halt and stare at a poster board that has been set up on an easel. It announces a new "adventure experience," as the poster board says, one that all guests are invited to attend. Only ten people at a time can go on an expedition, but the resort will offer multiple opportunities to participate during the coming days.

Emilio stands beside the easel, holding a clipboard and staring at whatever is written on the paper it holds.

I approach him. "Hi, Emilio."

His head pops up, and he smiles brightly. "Hey, Vanessa. How's your day going so far?"

"Fine, thank you." I point at the poster board. "What is zip-lining?"

"It's a fun and exciting way to experience the outdoors. You're strapped into a harness that hangs from a zip-line cable, and that line is strung up between trees, about seventy feet above the ground. So basically, you're flying through the air, though with a safety line. It's a great way to see the wildlife and the scenery."

"That does sound exciting." Just the idea of flying through the air on a length of cable makes me terrified and thrilled at the same time. I've never done anything that wild in my entire life. Maybe I need to take more risks and test my limits. "How do I sign up, Emilio?"

His eyes widen. "You want to go zip-lining?"

"Yes. Is there an age limit? You're staring at me like I must be insane."

"No, no, nothing like that. I'm just surprised because you seem like the sort who prefers to stay on the ground." He winces. "Sorry. I don't know you well enough to say something like that."

"It's okay. I'm not offended. Since I'm a science teacher and middle-aged, I can't blame you for assuming I wouldn't want to take a big risk." I glance at the poster board again, and the photo of a woman grinning while she's whisked through the treetops. "To be honest, I never would have come to a nudist resort if I hadn't won a free vacation to this place. Coming here has changed my mindset in a lot of ways."

"So, should I sign you up for the zip-line tour?"

"Yes, absolutely."

Emilio scrawls my name on the list on his clipboard. Then he gives me a brochure about zip lining. I will have my first-ever treetop adventure at three o'clock this afternoon. A sensation like a chill and a thrill mashed into one feeling rushes through me. I can't believe I'm doing this.

I whirl around, preparing to head for my suite.

But I slam into Craig.

He blinks rapidly, seeming a touch dazed. "Shit, Vanessa, I'm sorry. Didn't mean to crash into you."

"It's okay. I should have watched where I was going."

His gaze drops to my chest, but I doubt he's ogling my breasts. I'm sure he's squinting at the brochure I'm hugging to my chest, though he can't see much of it. His brows have wrinkled.

Craig leans sideways to peer at the poster board on the easel behind me. "You can't be going zip-lining."

"Why can't I? It's not like I have dementia and might fall off the zip line."

"I didn't mean it that way." He lifts his gaze to my face. "You're afraid of heights."

"No, I am not. Sometimes I get anxious in high places, but I tried exposure therapy about eighteen months ago, and it actually helped. Thought I might want to vacation in the Swiss Alps and go skiing. That meant I'd need to ride in a ski lift."

Craig's jaw falls open. "Every time I suggested we should go on a family ski vacation, you came up with a dozen reasons why we shouldn't do it."

He's not completely wrong. We never went skiing partly because of my anxiety about heights. But mostly, I worried about our kids getting hurt, and the idea of bunny slopes didn't ease my fears.

Time to fess up. "I've changed, Craig. That's another reason why I doubt we could become a couple again. You seem to still be stuck in your old ways."

"Old ways? I came to a nudist resort."

"But once you leave this place, you'll probably go back to the way you always were."

"You might too."

It would be great if he could stop making insightful comments. I'm trying to push him away, but he won't give up. The fact that he's right is both annoying and confusing. Will I go back to being a boring science teacher who instructs teenagers in how to dissect frogs? I don't want to be that woman anymore. I love my job, but I need more these days.

"You're right," I say. "Maybe I will go back to being boring old me, Mrs. Hathaway the science teacher."

"I thought you went back to using your maiden name."

"Um, yes, I did. But not at school. I didn't want to confuse my students by telling them they now need to call me Ms. Stendahl."

He crosses his arms over his chest. "Did you change your driver's license to say 'Stendahl'?"

"No."

"Why didn't you do that?"

I wish he would stop asking me questions. I could just tell him to buzz off, but I have an annoying habit of being honest and forthright. "I never got around to doing it, that's all."

"Why not?"

"Does it matter? I was busy, I guess. You know what the lines are like at the DMV."

"Uh-huh." He narrows his gaze on me. "But I think you're side-stepping, Vanessa. Why is it so hard to admit you wish we hadn't split up?"

"Why?" His question has ignited a spark of anger and pain that I'd tried to douse over the past three years. Now, it bursts into a bonfire. "Maybe I don't like to admit that because it's humiliating. You left me. That's not something I like to dwell on, and I sure as hell don't want to admit that I wish we hadn't divorced."

Craig lets his arms fall to his sides, and his expression has softened. He shakes his head slowly. "I know it was all my fault. I explained the reasons why I ended our marriage, and I can't think of any other way to say I'm sorry."

"I don't know what I feel right now. Please, just give me some time."

"Please, Vanessa, don't run away."

"Why not? You did." I hug the zip lining brochure to my chest more tightly, making the paper crinkle. "You abandoned me, and I don't know if I can ever move past that."

I whirl around and walk away.

Chapter Sixteen

Craig

As I watch Vanessa stalk off down the corridor, I experience a strong urge to beat myself in the head with a miniten thug. Why do I keep screwing up and making her feel bad? I want to make her happy. How a discussion about zip-lining turned into a painful argument about our divorce, I don't know. The situation spiraled out of control. That seems to happen a lot since I tricked my ex-wife into vacationing at a nudist resort.

Maybe I should have brought out the big guns, but that's one thing I've desperately tried to avoid discussing. Mentioning that might crack her shell open so we can have a real conversation, or it might send her running back to America. The risk is too great.

No, I can't bring up the fact that she moved out of our house before I even considered filing for divorce.

Vanessa had never cheated on me, and vice versa. I lost her because I was miserable in my work life and let that bleed into our family life.

I shuffle up to the poster board that rests on an easel. *Come join us for a zip lining adventure like no other*, the poster says. *Experience the adrenaline rush of soaring through the forest canopy.* I can see why Vanessa might like to try this extreme sport. She loves nature, and she seems to want to try new, exciting adventures. I do too—since I landed on this island.

Emilio walks up to me. "Want to join the zip-lining tour?"

I study the photos in the poster that depict naked adults having a great time, soaring through the forest, grinning and laughing. Vanessa wants to try zip lining. The least I can do is go along with her and show that I'm not a stuffy, middle-aged computer geek anymore. I can't change my age, but I can break out of my shell—for her.

"Yes, Emilio, I want to sign up for the zip-lining tour."

"Brilliant! I can fit you in for the three o'clock tour."

"Sounds perfect."

He gives me the same brochure Vanessa had been holding and instructs me to read everything. When I show up for the tour, I'll need to sign a waiver. Basically, I have to swear that I have no heart conditions or other medical issues that might endanger me during a zip-lining adventure. The waiver also includes a lengthy statement in which I absolve the resort of any liability if I should die or become injured while zip lining. Maybe that should bother me, but I've signed plenty of waivers in my life. I don't think twice about it anymore.

Back in my bungalow, I read the brochure to make sure I understand how the zip-lining thing will work. We will all be nude, sitting in a harness that's connected to the zip line. The resort recommends that we wear shoes, though that's not required.

Vanessa might be slightly annoyed when she finds out I'm going on the same zip-lining tour that she signed up for, but I can deal with her disapproval. I'd much rather handle her pleasure, though. I hope we can do some of that after our big adventure, but I won't hold my breath. She's always been a stubborn woman. I love that about her.

I decide against eating a snack before the zip-lining tour. Motion sickness has never been an issue for me, but then, I've never soared through the forest canopy before. The brochure instructed guests to gather on the main patio. From there, we will be led into the woods, to the starting point for our adventure.

We will climb up the mountain.

That sounds like quite a workout, but the brochure stated that we would ride in ORVs partway up the mountain. Then we will walk the rest of the way. I think I can handle that. They wouldn't let people older than me go on this expedition if they knew it would be a tough hike.

Or maybe I'm just hoping that's their plan.

I spend the next half hour searching the internet for information about the tall, craggy mountain that sits in the exact center of the island. Heirani Motu is the name of the island, but I have no idea what they call the mountain. Maybe it shares the same name with the island itself. Finally, I stumble onto a geology website set up by an Australian university, which tells me that the name of the peak is Beautiful Mountain in English, but I won't even attempt to pronounce the Maori version.

At five minutes to three, I stride out onto the main patio.

I see people I've met over the past few days and say hello to them. But my focus is on Vanessa. She's talking to James and Holly Bythesea, who will take us as far as the base of the mountain, where the ORVs are parked. From there, Emilio and Rene will guide us, along with the zip-lining experts who will be waiting for us at the designated spot.

My ex-wife doesn't notice me as I approach her and Emilio.

"Hey, Vanessa, are you ready for the big adventure?"

She jumps and gapes at me. "Craig? What are you doing here?"

"Emilio told me about the zip-lining adventure, and I thought it sounded like a great way to see more of the island."

"Did you." That was not a question. She's using her stern teacher voice now, and oddly, it makes me hot for her. "What a coincidence. You just happen to sign up for the same event that I picked."

"No, it wasn't an accident. I saw you with the brochure, remember?"

"Of course I remember. But I didn't think—Never mind. We won't see each other once we're up in the trees. Right, Emilio?"

The poor guy grimaces and glances back and forth between me and Vanessa. "Well, I, ah...don't know the details of how it will work. You'll need to ask the experts."

"They aren't here yet," I say. "The brochure says we'll meet up with them at the base of the mountain trail."

"Yeah, that's right." Emilio seems desperately relieved that I changed the subject. He checks his watch, then clears his throat. "I need to meet up with Rene to get the ORVs. I'll see you in a bit."

"Come on, everyone," James shouts. "It's time to head for the trail."

Aside from me and Vanessa, our group includes ten other guests including Zach and Aspen. It's a short hike from the resort proper to the trailhead, and we arrive before Rene and Emilio. James hiked up the trail wearing business-casual clothes while Holly looks like a sexy, professional woman. Emilio and Rene wore clothes too.

That fact makes me curious, and I can't resist asking a question. "I guess all the resort staff keep their clothes on at all times, huh?"

James lifts one brow. "Is that what you think? No, we remain clothed during work hours, but all staff are permitted to go nude in their off time if they so choose."

Holly grins. "James loves to sunbathe in the nude and make love on the beach too."

James rolls his eyes at her. "For pity's sake, Holly. Must we share everything with our guests?"

"Everybody will figure it out once you strip naked on the beach tomorrow." She winks at me. "That's our day off."

"You guys deserve a break, for sure," I say. "Seems like you work twenty-four seven."

"Not quite. James used to be a workaholic, but I cured him of that."

I'm probably making a pained face. "I've been a workaholic too. That's part of the reason Vanessa and I broke up."

"We didn't break up, Craig. You dumped me."

Vanessa's voice makes me spin around and stare at her. "Hey, Nessa. Ready for our zip-lining adventure?"

"You make it sound like we'll be zip-lining as a couple. We won't. I'm going solo."

I've always been impressed with the way she can be stern while still speaking in a calm tone. It's a mom thing, I guess.

Engine noises grumble in the distance, growing louder swiftly. Then two identical odd-looking vehicles emerge from another trail and stop nearby. I can see the men who drove the vehicles—Rene the pilot and Emilio the assistant manager. They both grin as they hop out of their contraptions.

"How do ya like our ORVs?" Emilio shouts. "We'll be riding them up the mountain to the starting point for the zip-line tour."

I thought "ORV" was just a fancier name for ATVs. But no, it's clearly a different animal. The ORVs in question look like a cross between a dune buggy and a jeep, without any of the amenities, including a distinct lack of windows or seatbelts. Well, I guess they do have doors, of a sort. That must be what the canvas slings on each side of the vehicle are supposed to be.

"We are not ready to go yet," James declares, loudly. "I haven't given my speech. Please gather round and hold any questions until I've finished."

Holly grins and kisses his cheek. "You are so cute when you get general-manager-y."

Vanessa has never called me "cute." But then, she isn't in her twenties. I love that Vanessa is mature, and I'm very glad my days of dating silly young women are long gone.

James gives a professional speech, advising us of the rules for this expedition and explaining how everything will unfold. When I'd booked a nudist vacation for me and Vanessa, I'd assumed this place would be more like a hippie commune than a five-star resort. I was dead wrong. They might cater to the au naturel set, but all the employees take their jobs seriously.

"And now, it's time to send you on your way," James announces. "Emilio and Rene, we are handing the reins over to you gents. And to all of you, our wonderful guests, enjoy your adventure."

Holly and James wave goodbye as they amble off down the trail.

"All right, listen up," Emilio shouts. "Five of you will get into each of the ORVs. I'll drive the first one, and Rene will follow us in the second one."

Rene grins with devilish delight. "First come, first served, mates. Hand-to-hand combat is allowed, so start fighting for the spot right next to the partner of your choice."

Emilio shakes his head and rolls his eyes. "There will be no fighting. Rene has a bizarre sense of humor."

The first ORV gets filled up first. I try to snag a spot in that one, since Vanessa is riding in it, but a pair of senior citizens beat me to it. I wind up in the backseat of the second ORV, squashed between Zach and Aspen. She starts chattering away at me, but as soon as the engines rev up, I can't hear whatever she might be saying.

Our trip up the mountain is noisy, but not deafening. The bumps aren't too bumpy either. I imagine the resort staff made sure the trail would be relatively smooth for those of us who aren't strapping young twenty-somethings.

We arrive at our destination to find two people, a man and a woman, waiting for us. These must be the experts who will oversee our zip-lining adventure. At least they both look mature enough to know what they're doing.

The woman waves her arms to get our attention. "Listen up! Your zip-lining tour is about to begin. I know you've all signed waivers, but we need to go through the safety measure just to be sure."

Her accent reminds me of Emilio, so she must be from New Zealand too.

"My name is Mila Baker," our hostess declares. "And this hand-some chap beside me is my husband, Cooper. We'll be guiding you on this tour. If you have any questions, please don't hesitate to speak up. Now, here comes the bloody boring part."

She recites the rules and explains how zip-lining works, then shows us a harness. We will be strapped into one of those. Cooper tells us all about hand braking, which is how we can slow down our speed while zip-lining. He and Mila give each of us a pair of sturdy leather gloves. Those are our brakes. Cooper tells us about the potential dangers of hand braking. We all go through several rounds of practicing our braking skills with a short zip line that's about six feet above the ground.

"There will be five zip lines," Cooper tells us. "Four for you lot, and one for Mila and me in case we need to quickly reach someone who's in trouble. We've been doing this for twelve years and have never had a serious problem. But if you're at all anxious about this, don't be shy about speaking up."

Zach laughs. "Seriously? We're all standing here buck naked. Do you really think we're shy?"

Cooper smiles. "Point taken."

He and Mila are clothed, just like James, Holly, Emilio, and Rene.

Our ORV drivers wish us "a bloody fantastic time," then head back down the mountain.

"Ready for a hike?" Mila asks. "It's not far to the top of the zip line, and the grade is pretty gentle. Let's go."

Mila and Cooper guide us up a narrower trail that's wide enough for only two people to walk side by side. I try to get close to Vanessa, but she sees me coming and scoots ahead to walk beside Aspen. I find myself shoulder to shoulder with Zach. Fortunately, he doesn't talk. He does, however, keep bumping his shoulder into mine while grinning and winking at me. I have no idea what that means, but I decide to assume he's just excited about zip-lining.

I'm getting a pit in my stomach that grows every minute.

We reach the top of the trail, about halfway up the mountain, and stop. I can see sturdy trees with zip lines attached to them. I can also see the mechanisms that make the zip line work, though I don't know the official terms for them. Mila shows us the "swing seat" that each of us will ride in, and then there are trolleys and carabiners and bungee brakes and various other things I know I'll never remember once I'm flying through the air. Luckily, I don't need to remember. Mila and Cooper tell us they've installed automatic braking systems too that will make sure we never get going too fast.

"Remember," Cooper says, "you can always brake by using your hands. Just make sure you're wearing gloves. If you chose no gloves, then don't attempt active braking."

His stern tone convinced me. Whether the younger folks here listen, only time will tell. I'm sure Zach and Aspen will heed the warnings. They're not stupid or reckless.

"We're running four lines for you lot," Mila reminds us. "But Cooper and I will be watching out for you in case anyone gets in trouble. Now, who wants to go first?"

Zach and Aspen thrust their hands up and wave frenetically.

Then Vanessa raises her hand.

I see another guy vacillating, seeming like he's about to take the last spot on the first run. *Oh, hell no.* If my wife is out there, I'm going with her. I thrust my hand up and shout, "Me too!"

Yeah, I've gone completely insane.

Chapter Seventeen

Vanessa

Craig followed me on this crazy tour, but I assumed he would back out once it came time to actually climb onto a zip line. He doesn't like heights any more than I do. When we visited the Empire State Building, he couldn't even go out on the observation deck. Yet here he is, volunteering to fly through the trees with a single cable to hold him up. Granted, Mila and Cooper told us our lines are made with galvanized aircraft cable. That sounds very tough.

I keep glancing at Craig while Mila and Cooper get the four of us fitted with swing seats and demonstrate the active braking method again. I still keep expecting my ex-husband to chicken out. But instead, he grins at me and gives me the thumbs-up sign. Did an alien take possession of his body? I can't believe anything else would make him participate in zip lining.

Zach takes off first, followed swiftly by Aspen.

During the safety speech, Cooper had mentioned that the resort planted wireless cameras throughout the zip-lining path, so they can rescue anyone who panics. The cameras will also take photos of us. That information was included in the waiver. The resort crew seems to have taken every precaution while still ensuring we have a good time.

Now it's time for me and Craig to take off. My tummy flutters. Every hair on my body stiffens. I'm excited and terrified at the same time, but I won't back out. I need to push my limits and find out what I'm made of.

"Ready to go, Nessa? Or are you too scared?"

I glance at Craig again, and his grin gets even bigger. "If you can handle it, I can for sure."

"Let's find out, huh?"

Mila gives him a gentle push, and he starts rolling down the zip line.

Cooper gives me a push, and suddenly, I'm soaring over the landscape with blue sky above me and nothing but air beneath me. A tingle of excitement sweeps over me. The freedom and thrill of it all robs me of breath for a moment, then I suck in a big lungful and whoop.

Craig has slowed down, apparently to wait for me to catch up.

As I glide past him, he pulls his hands away from the cable and rushes after me. I whoop again, and he joins me this time, our cries of joy echoing through the forest canopy. A brightly colored parrot flies out of the treetops and soars past us close enough that I can hear its wings flapping. Our guides had told us the zip line goes down at a six-percent grade, but it feels like more than that. Adrenaline sings in my veins, heightening my excitement until I feel like I could fly away with that parrot.

I throw my arms out and shriek with joy. I'm too old to behave this way, aren't I? Oh, who gives a damn. I've never experienced anything like this before, and I plan to soak up every last drop of adrenaline and then some.

Craig's laughter echoes off the trees along with mine.

When we reach the first trolley, a bungee brake stops us, but only long enough for us to catch our breath. I see Cooper on the next line over, and he instructs us in how to switch to the next section of the line. Beyond his shoulder, I glimpse Mila doing the same for Zach and Aspen.

"The first waterfall is coming up," Cooper hollers to us. "We might see some wildlife there. The island has flying foxes, which are fruit bats, as well as mongooses. Of course, we also have lots of birds and sea life."

"But we can't see the marine life on this tour."

He grins. "Wait until the last leg of your zip line adventure."

"Are mongooses native to this island?"

"No. They were brought here by the Europeans who settled on the island for a while. But those blokes gave up and went to South America instead. That's the story I heard, at any rate."

We continue down the mountain, moving slower in areas where we want to get a better view of the terrain and search for wildlife, then going faster in spots that seem perfect for a quick zip. I love it when we race across a gully with the blue sky above us. When I whoop, Craig does too. We glance at each other and grin. But when we reach the waterfall, we use our gloved hands to stop and study the area below us.

A rainbow forms right in front of us. I gaze at it with a kind of wonder I haven't experienced since I was a little girl. The full rainbow has colors brighter than any I've seen before, and when a white bird flies by, I get a lump in my throat. It's just that beautiful.

"Look, Nessa, it's a double rainbow now."

Craig's words make me sit up straighter in my swing seat and search for what he saw. But he's a little ways ahead of me. Maybe I'm not in the right position.

He waves to me. "Come on, slide down here. You'll miss the double rainbow if you don't hurry."

I release my hold on my line and slide down toward Craig. He grabs my arm as I'm about to glide right past him. I grip my line with both hands and stare at the gorgeous double rainbow in front of me. I've never seen anything like it. The colors are so vivid, and it feels like I could reach out and touch it.

Craig pulls me closer and whispers into my ear, "Do you think that's some kind of sign? A double rainbow while we're both hanging here."

I hear what he said, but I can't think about what it means. My focus remains bound to the bright, arching lines in the air while they gradually fade away. Once the rainbow has vanished, I turn to Craig. "What did you say?"

"Maybe that was a sign, something to show us the way."

"The way to what?"

"Back to each other."

My throat tightens. I stare at him for several seconds, and though I want to tell him that's bullshit, I can't make my vocal cords work. So, I take the coward's way out. I release my hand, letting my trolley rush down the line away from him.

He catches up to me but doesn't try to have a conversation. Though he does glance at me and keeps pace with me, my ex-husband seems to have given up on the idea that a rainbow is some kind of miracle that will heal our relationship.

Whether I want to heal it, I still don't know.

I hear whoops and shrieks, and when I glance in that direction, I see Aspen and Zach hurtling down their lines. They're having a great time. I was too until Craig said that thing about the rainbow. I can't even think the words anymore. My brain refuses to let me. Or maybe it's my heart urging me to forget.

Why has Craig never chastised me for moving out of our house before he filed for divorce?

The thought stops me. I grab onto my zip line and literally stop now, staring down at the forest floor, so far below me.

Craig halts his line beside me. "Vanessa, what's wrong?"

I can't respond. My mind has completely frozen up, like a computer with a glitch. My gaze remains aimed down at the ground, but I don't see anything. My thoughts have retreated so deeply that I've become immobilized.

"Wake up, Vanessa." Craig grabs my line and shakes it. "Wake up. Are you having a panic attack?"

I manage to shake my head. My throat is still too tight for me to speak. But my lips begin to tremble, my eyes burn, and I know that any second I'll start to cry. This is insane. I can't hang here on a zip line while sobbing.

Craig takes hold of my seat and pulls me closer. "Snap out of it, Vanessa."

All I can do is shake my head.

"I can't leave you like this. But I can't think of anything to do to help you except for…"

He moves his hand to my nape, tips my head back, and kisses me. His lips feel warm and soft, and they taste like mint lip balm. My eyes drift closed. My entire body slackens, though I manage to keep hold of my line so I won't start sliding down it again. Everything inside me turns warm and liquid. I lean into him while he slips his tongue between my lips to tease me with light flicks. I moan and let my jaw fall open just enough that I can thrust my tongue more deeply into his mouth, and we begin to ravish each other with slow, sensual movements.

Then he pulls away. "Feeling better?"

I blink several times quickly. Though I'd love to deny it, I need to tell him the truth. "Yes, I feel much better. Thank you."

"Why did you go catatonic?"

"Not sure." Of course I'm sure. I turned into a high-flying vegetable because I remembered the fact I had tried to forget for so long, the truth that my mind urged me to trap inside the deepest dungeon inside me. "That's a lie. I do know why I froze. It's because I was the one who walked out on our marriage, and I've felt guilty for blaming you. Sure, you filed for divorce, but I started the ball rolling."

He cups my cheek. "We're both to blame. What we need to do is talk about all of that so we can find out how to repair our relationship. I still love you, Nessa. I always will love you."

I can't speak, but only because I don't want to give him false hope. At least I'm not catatonic anymore.

Craig kisses me sweetly, then releases his hold on his zip line. I watch him glide downward for a few seconds, then release my line too and rush down after him. I catch up just as we slow down, thanks to the slope of our lines becoming shallower, and I flash him a quick smile. He returns the gesture. Then we both need to concentrate on switching to the next switchover. By the time we reach the end of our aerial adventure, we're both exhausted in the best way.

Mila and Cooper arrived just before us. Aspen and Zach have already gotten out of their gear, but Craig and I need a little help. Once we're free, we both sit down on the ground to rest and watch the others come flying down the mountain four at a time. The oldest zip-liners in our group are a married couple in their seventies, who surprise everyone with their derring-do. Cooper announces that those two had beaten everyone, sliding down the mountain faster than anyone else and with amazing finesse.

Getting older isn't such a bad thing after all.

Once we've all recovered from the excitement, we head back down the trail to the spot where we had started. Rene and Emilio are waiting for us in the ORVs. And soon, we're riding back down the mountain to the trailhead. After that, we go our separate ways.

Despite being tired, I feel wonderful.

Until Craig catches up to me. "Should we talk about your revelation?"

"Not now. I need to let it sink into my brain. I swear that's not an excuse."

"I believe you." He tentatively clasps my hand. "Want to have dinner at my place tonight?"

"Where is your suite? You never said."

"I don't have a suite. It's a little bungalow around the back of the main building. Couldn't afford lavish accommodations."

Suddenly, I realize I've threaded my fingers with his, but I have no desire to pull my hand away. "I'd love to see where you've been sleeping."

"Right now? Or later?"

"I could eat a four-course feast after all the excitement."

He lifts our joined hands, kissing my knuckles. "Then let's go straight to my place."

Chapter Eighteen

Craig

I hope you're not getting the wrong idea," Vanessa says as we swerve down the path that bypasses the main building. "We are not going to have sex tonight. This is strictly for conversation and food, nothing else. Nod your head if you understand, Craig. You aren't nodding. Maybe I need to find a ruler and smack the back of your hand with it."

"Is that how you deal with students who annoy you? I thought you were anti-corporal punishment."

"Yes. But I'll make an exception for you."

"We are going to talk and eat. If you can't keep your hands off me, that won't be my fault."

She slaps my ass. "You never used to be so contrary."

"Things change." I reclaim her hand as we veer down another path to avoid the curving swimming pool. "I remember when we were first married, and we couldn't get enough of each other."

"Yeah, I remember that too. It was a long time ago. Everything is different now."

We've just reached my bungalow, and I open the door, gesturing for Vanessa to go inside. "You said you regret moving out of our house."

"I regret being the one who moved out. At the time, I was sure I was doing the right thing for both of us."

As I shut the door, she turns toward me and sighs. "Now you want to talk."

"You say that like I'm forcing you to give a speech on Victorian etiquette." I lay a hand on her back, leading her to the little sofa in the living area. It's just big enough for two people, with one cushion separating us. "Sit down, Vanessa. I really want us to talk about everything, no interruptions this time."

"Agreed." She settles onto the sofa. "Let's talk about why we split up."

"Okay." I sit down and angle toward her. "Why did you move out? You said you needed space, but you would never explain what that meant. I didn't want to ask too many questions."

"Why? You were never shy about that."

"I was afraid I'd lose you forever if I asked too many questions. But I realize now that I should have pushed for an explanation."

She tucks her legs beneath her and rubs her arms. "Is that why you filed for divorce? You were afraid to ask questions?"

"Well, not entirely. That was a big part of it, though." I take a moment to think about how to explain this without sounding like a moron. Then again, I need to be honest, which means telling her everything, even the humiliating parts. "We hadn't been intimate in a couple of years. I assumed you'd lost interest, and then I saw you with that guy from your school."

"What guy?"

"Uh, the one who used to stop by the house once in a while to talk to you about school stuff."

"Peter?" She laughs. "Did you think I was having an affair with him? He's the school principal. Peter had gotten a job offer from a private school and wanted to know if I would take on the principal position when he left. I didn't really want the job. He was determined to talk me into tossing my hat into the ring for the selection committee. But that's all it was."

"Oh. I see." Now I really do feel like a moron. "I thought you might have been talking to that guy because you wanted out of our marriage. I never for one second believed you were cheating on me. But you might have been...looking at all your options."

She stares at me for a moment, then shakes her head. "Honestly, Craig, why didn't you talk to me about this at the time?"

Now that I've thoroughly embarrassed myself, might as well keep going. "Since the day we met, I've known I don't deserve you, Vanessa. You're smart, beautiful, accomplished, loved by your students. What you do makes a difference in the world. I've always had tech jobs. That means I sit around all day staring at a computer screen. I'm not exciting to be with."

"That's baloney. Do you think I married you out of pity? I loved you, Craig. You are just as smart and accomplished as I am."

"You don't understand." I rub the back of my neck, lowering my gaze so I won't need to look her in the eye. "I was sick of my job. But that's not the worst problem. I, uh, also...got laid off six months ago."

"What? Why?"

I shrug. "The company needed to downsize, and the older employees are always the first to go. I'm not young and fresh anymore, that's what my boss told me. I'm too stuck in my ways."

"When we first met, you loved your job. It was exciting to be on the cutting edge of technology. That's what you told me."

"And it was true back then. But over the years, I've had to keep learning new skills to stay current, and the pace of new technologies has been hectic." I slump into my corner of the little sofa. "It's exhausting. And finally, I couldn't keep up anymore. My boss told me so. The younger employees have a better grasp on the cutting-edge stuff."

Vanessa slides closer to me, laying a hand on my knee. "I wish I'd known all of that while we were still married. I'm so sorry I wasn't there for you when you got laid off."

"It's no wonder you don't want to come back to me. I'm a loser."

"No, I would never call you that. Remember when I was working at a private school and it went out of business? You supported me emotionally and financially until I found another job."

"We supported each other. That's what marriage is about. Joint bank accounts, joint lives, joint everything. But I guess that's an old-fashioned world view."

"Maybe. But it's what I loved most about our marriage."

Talking to Vanessa, I realize that I've been a complete idiot and a jackass. I hated my job, so I divorced my wife. After everything I just told her, she must think I'm a pathetic lump of a man.

"Don't you want to know why I moved out of the house?"

Her question jerks me out of my self-pitying thoughts, and I meet her gaze. "Of course I want to know."

"We had been drifting apart for a while, and like you said, we stopped being intimate. But the last straw was when I suggested we should go on vacation to someplace tropical and finally have the honeymoon we never had." She leans toward me, her gaze nailed to mine. "But you said that was a waste of money. I practically begged you to go away with me. It felt like you didn't want me anymore, and moving out seemed like the best way to get your attention."

I wince. "You were expecting me to run after you, weren't you? But instead, I filed for divorce."

"Men are emotional infants. Every woman knows that. None of you have any clue how to handle relationships."

"Why are you suddenly giving me an out? An excuse for my behavior?"

"Because I've realized we both made mistakes that hurt each other." She wriggles even closer. "When I was hanging from that zip line, having the best time of my life, I suddenly realized that I was having fun because you were with me."

Should I tell her now about my grand deception? That she's only on this island because I maneuvered her to this place? No, it's too soon. Vanessa only just realized she shouldn't have moved out of our house and that she had fun because I was with her. This vacation means nothing if I'm not with my wife. Ex-wife. I need to be careful how I break the news to her.

"I loved zip-lining with you," I tell her. "Never saw you that happy before. But I know I have a lot of work ahead of me to show you I'll never walk away again."

"Let's forget about that for now. I'm starving."

"Then let's order room service."

Despite our serious conversation, once our food arrives, we enjoy more than good eats. We joke with each other and laugh about how crazy it is that two middle-aged people have come to a nudist resort. This is how we used to be. During our marriage, until things gradually disintegrated, we laughed and talked and made love and took care of our kids. We were a family. But more than that, we were a couple in love, and for years, we stayed that way.

I hardly noticed when the downward spiral began, not until it was too late.

We ordered dessert too. Vanessa had requested that I choose the dessert and make it something "deliciously sinful and dripping with yumminess." I didn't use those exact words when I placed our order. Only a woman would say something like that. But I managed to get the point across to Danielle, the resort employee who took our order.

But the way Vanessa had spoken those words... Damn, it made me horny as hell.

Now that we've finished our main course, it's time for dessert. Vanessa also commanded me to order at least three desserts that matched her criteria. So, we wound up with wine glasses filled with strawberry cheesecake mousse, red wine lollipops, and cherry bombs. I wasn't sure what those things were, but I trusted Danielle to choose romantic sweets for us. She did a bang-up job, for sure. Now I know what a cherry bomb is—chocolate cake balls with a cherry in the center and a dark chocolate coating around the whole thing. The cherry stems poke out of the balls.

I'd kept the desserts hidden until after our meal. Now, I lift the dome lid and reveal the sensual goodies to Vanessa.

She rubs her palms together and licks her lips with one long, slow glide of her tongue. "Mm, you did good, Craig. These look incredible."

I love the sultry tone of her voice. But if she keeps talking that way and devouring the desserts with her gaze, I might snap and fuck her right here on this tiny sofa. "Which dessert do you want first?"

"Maybe I'll start with a cherry bomb." Her focus shifts to my lap, and her lips curve into a sexy smile. "Or something bigger and meatier."

She licks her lips again, exposing more of her tongue while she swipes it over her upper lip.

Meatier? Even I'm not dense enough to misunderstand that comment.

Vanessa plucks up a cherry bomb and places it delicately on her tongue. When she seals her lips around the confection, only the stem is still visible. She half closes her eyes and moans, the sound so throaty and erotic that my dick jerks. She puckers her lips and pulls the stem free, then begins to chew the candy in a leisurely manner, like she wants to savor it for as long as possible.

Finally, she swallows and opens her eyes. "You should try one of these. Take it into your mouth and let the sweetness and dark chocolate melt away your inhibitions."

"Are you trying to seduce me, Nessa?"

"What if I am?" She plucks a glass of raspberry cheesecake off the tray and grabs a spoon. Once she's loaded up the spoon, she holds it to my mouth. "Imagine this is what I taste like."

Oh yeah, she is definitely trying to seduce me.

I close my mouth around the spoonful of pink mousse and let her slowly pull the spoon free. I take a page from her book and consume the confection as if I plan to spend an hour savoring that one mouthful. Then I groan deeply.

"You're getting me so turned on, Craig."

"Mm, that was good." I wipe my mouth with one finger, letting bits of the dessert cling to the tip, and offer it to her. "But nothing on earth could ever taste as delicious as you."

Vanessa flicks her tongue over my fingertip, lapping up the remnants of my raspberry cheesecake mousse. "What should we do now?"

"Get dirty, sweaty, and thoroughly satisfied."

Chapter Nineteen

Vanessa

I would love to do that," I tell Craig as I slide even closer to him, and our bodies brush against each other. My breathing grows heavier just from that simple touch. "Why did we never do anything like this while we were married? I think this island has magical powers to make everyone horny."

He chuckles. "I think we've both realized, finally, that we are not the same two people who got married and had kids. We're mature adults who do whatever the hell we want."

"That's true. We love our kids, but this is the time in our lives when we get to cut loose and try new things. Getting older isn't a bad thing." I slide a hand up his thigh, rewarded by the way he sucks in a sharp breath. "We're footloose and fancy free now."

"Does anyone still use that term?"

"Only old fogies like us."

He grasps my waist and pulls me onto his lap, where his erection presses against my belly. "Age does have its benefits. We don't need condoms, and we can explore any kind of adventurous sex that we want."

"How adventurous do you want to be?"

"Tell me your fantasies, the ones you never would have admitted to having back when we were married."

I bite the inside of my lip while I gaze into his eyes and consider my options. "I'd love to start with eating dessert off each other's bodies, then move on to something wilder."

"Dessert we can do for sure. What sort of wilder things did you have in mind?"

How far should I go with this? We both want to get closer, and we also both want to try new sexual experiences. Our marriage had been a happy one, and we had a decent sex life for most of that time. But I know we can do better. It all depends on how much we're willing to push our limits.

Craig is the only man I would ever want to do this with.

So, I slide deeper into his lap, lifting my hips just enough to seat his cock firmly beneath my cleft. "How about a little bondage?"

"Are you serious? The schoolteacher wants to get tied up? Or maybe you want to tie me up."

"Either. Both. I just want to try something new. Are you game?"

"For you, I'll try anything." He stands up while I still have my legs wrapped around him, then sets me down. "Maybe we should do this in your suite. It's bigger and has more opportunities for getting down and dirty."

"Good idea."

"And besides, my bungalow must seem like a slum compared to your suite."

Is that why he hadn't invited me here until tonight? He thinks I'm a snob. Well, it's probably more accurate to say he worries I'll think less of him. To reassure him, I clasp his face with both hands, tugging gently until he dips his head toward mine. "I would have sex with you in a pup tent if that was the only option. The place doesn't matter as long as we're together."

"Yeah, I knew you wouldn't care about my little bungalow. The problem was me." He grasps my ass in both hands. "I'm over that now."

"Glad to hear it. Let's take our food back to my suite."

He picks up the tray full of goodies, and I open the door for him. Once we reach my suite, I order us a bottle of champagne too. Only then do we realize there's a slight hitch in our erotic plans for the evening.

Craig smacks his forehead. "Oh, no. How can we do bondage fun without the bondage gear? I think the gift shop carries that kind of stuff, but it's too late for that. The shop is closed for the night."

Our plans have skidded to a halt before we even really got started. Or have they? I suddenly get an idea. "Maybe I should call Holly and ask her."

"You want to tell the guest services manager that we need bondage gear?"

"If that makes you uncomfortable, we can delay our plans until tomorrow night."

He grabs my cell phone off the nightstand and hands it to me. "Call Holly. I can't wait another day."

"Neither can I." My fingers fumble as I dial Holly's number, which was included in the phone list in our welcome packets. I want to do this with Craig so badly that I've turned clumsy. At last, I manage to dial the right numbers. "Hi, Holly, sorry to bother you after hours. But Craig and I could, um, use your help. It's a delicate matter."

"What's wrong?"

"Nothing. But we decided to try a bit of light bondage, and we suddenly realized we don't have the right equipment for that. Could you let us into the gift shop?"

"Oh, you don't need to go there. Are you guys in your suite or Craig's bungalow?"

"My suite."

"Perfect. Stay where you are. I'll bring everything you need."

She hangs up before I can ask what it is she thinks we need. Bondage paraphernalia, I assume. But she talked like someone who's had experience with this kind of thing before. James and Holly do have that vibe sometimes.

"What should we do while we wait?" Craig asks. "I guess we could sit on the bed or go out onto the patio."

Someone knocks on the door.

I rush over to swing it open. "Holly? Wow, that was fast."

"Told you I'd bring everything you might need." She offers me a paper grocery bag. "This should do the trick. James and I like to get a little kinky sometimes. My hubby insisted that we should give you guys this stuff, and we'll order new gear. It's our gift to you. But don't worry, the vibrator is brand new and has never been used."

"That's very generous. Thank you."

"James and I agree that you and Craig are a great couple, and we want to do whatever we can to help you reconcile." She thrusts the bag at me again, leaning in to whisper, "Have fun."

Holly trots off down the corridor.

I shut the door and hold up the bag. "We have our gear. Are you ready to try something totally new to us?"

"Absolutely."

We sit down on the bed and peruse the items Holly had brought for us. Soft ropes. Padded handcuffs. A blindfold. A vibrator. Edible underwear. She also included a book of sex positions. When I pull out that book, we exchange awkward glances, like teenage virgins who are about to screw for the first time. Then I flip the book open and skim the pages.

He drops his finger onto the book. "Stop there. The Amazon position looks interesting."

Yes, the sex manual has illustrations.

"Okay," I tell him. "We will start with dessert, then move on to the Amazon."

"Sounds like we're flying to South America."

"I hope we'll be flying high on endorphines very soon." I take one last look at the illustration, then shut the book. "Lie down, Craig. I'm going to eat you up."

He scuttles backward and turns lengthwise on the bed, resting his head on one of the plush pillows.

I crawl across the bed to kneel between his thighs. "How flexible are you?"

"Flexible? Not sure. I don't do yoga like you." He lifts his brows. "Are you still doing that?"

"Yes. You know I've always loved yoga." I rest my hands on his thighs, skating them up and down. "Let's give this position a try. If it's too difficult for you, just tell me so. That book offers tons of possibilities."

"I'd love to try something new. You never know, I might be more flexible than either of us knows."

"You're much more adventurous than you used to be. I love that."

"Never imagined either of us would go zip-lining, but I'm glad we did."

"Me too." I pat his thighs. "Now, bend your knees and bring them up to your chest."

He obeys my command without any hesitation or complaint. We had never been a bickering couple, not even when we broke up. But I love that we're developing a deeper kind of intimacy and trying new things together.

I watch him pull his knees up until they're almost touching his chest. "Wow, I'm impressed. You're very flexible. Are you sure you've never done yoga?"

"Positive. But I, ah, did start practicing tai chi. It's supposed to make you feel more balanced and relaxed, but maybe it can also improve flexibility."

"With you, it definitely has."

Craig practices tai chi? I can't believe it, but I'm glad he's been trying to find ways to alleviate stress. He'd gotten tense toward the end of our marriage.

I crawl forward until his legs cradle my hips. His cock lies nestled under me. I gently reposition it until the head nudges my entrance, then slowly push my hips forward. His length slides into me inch by inch, every sensation heightened by the thrill of trying something new, and I swear I can feel every millimeter of him. My breaths shorten. My flesh tingles everywhere that his cock touches me. I bite down on my bottom lip. Our gazes are bound to each other while he gradually fills me up to the hilt.

"Fuck, Vanessa, this is already the hottest thing we've ever done."

"Mm, I love it too."

He lays his hands on my upper thighs while I begin to rock forward and back, forward and back, moaning because it feels incredible. I peel his hands away from my thighs and lean forward as I place his palms on my breasts. He gently squeezes them and flicks his fingers over the tips, making me gasp.

"I don't want to come yet, Vanessa. But I want you to come."

"Anything you want to do to me, I want it too." I crawl backward so he can lower his legs. "I can't tell you how many times I fantasized about trying more adventurous things in bed. Just thinking about what you might do me gets me so turned on that my cream is dribbling down my inner thighs."

"I've always loved the flavor of you, but tonight, I want to devour you completely."

"Oh God, keep saying dirty things like that."

Craig sits up and leans over to grab the sex manual and flip through it. He stops on a particular page, gazing up at me with his head still bowed, and his mouth curls into the sexiest devilish grin I've ever seen. "Oh, I have a great idea."

"Do it. I'm up for anything with you."

"This will come in two stages, just like you."

He waddles around me and pats my bottom. "Lie down on your back, Nessa, please."

"Your polite commands make me even hotter."

"And your excited expression does the same to me. You really want to do this, and I love that."

He's excited about his great idea too, and I love that he wants to get playful and naughty with me. Maybe incredible sex won't instantly repair our relationship, but it just might open the door.

Craig snatches the paper bag off the floor and digs out the items he needs—several ropes. While I lie back on the bed, my head on the pillow, he sets the ropes out beside me and considers them, seeming like he's working out the best arrangement for tying me up. God, I want him to do that. What's wrong with two consenting adults having some filthy fun? My only regret is that we didn't try this years ago.

He picks up a rope and kneels between my feet. "Lift your legs as high as you comfortably can, at either side of your body."

As I follow his command, I realize all those yoga lessons had done some good. I can stretch my legs toward my body much further than I would have expected.

Craig ties one end of a long rope to my left ankle, then loops it through the headboard slats and ties the end to my right ankle. "Is this too tight?"

"No, it's perfect."

"Grasp your ankles."

He watches while I do that, licking his lips. Once I've done what he told me to do, he uses two shorter ropes to tie my wrists to my ankles. I am now spread-eagled with my legs almost touching my shoulders. Craig reaches into the bag again and pulls out a vibrator that has a curving shape.

The second he flicks the power switch, my pulse revs up.

But when he touches the vibrator to my folds, I jerk and gasp.

He pulls the device away. "Is that an 'oh please don't stop' gasp?"

"Yes, of course, yes."

"Good."

He drags the vibrator's tip up and down my cleft with such delicacy and slowness that my breaths quicken and my heart pounds. I try to writhe, but I can't, not with the ropes holding me in place. They're so soft that, whenever the ropes brush against my skin, I throw my head back and make desperate little noises. He drags the vibrator up my belly, carefully avoiding my clit, and places the head of the device over my pubic bone. Then he turns up the vibrations.

I cry out as my clit throbs.

"How badly do you need to come, Nessa?"

"So badly. Please, make me come."

He gives me that sexy, devilish grin again. Then he drops onto his belly and shimmies toward me until his face hovers directly in front of my sex. He licks his lips again. The vibrator is still humming away, though no longer touching my body. My pulse thunders in my ears because I need to come so badly, but at the same time, I never want him to stop. It's insane, but I don't care.

Craig thrusts the vibrator inside me, cranking it up to the highest setting, and seals his mouth over my clit. While he sucks and licks and nips at my nub, he keeps thrusting the vibrator in and out, deep and hard. The combination of those two sensations hurls me off that cliff. My entire body goes rigid, and I can feel my inner muscles pulsating around the vibrator while he pinches my clit with his teeth and consumes me like he never wants to stop feasting on me.

The pleasure barrels through me with such ferocity and heat that I can't even scream. I throw my head back and ride out the ecstasy.

Craig shuts off the vibrator and tosses it onto the mattress beside me. When he sits back on his heels, the full length of his cock bounces up and down, the crown rosy red and glistening with moisture that I desperately want to lick off it. His dick is the most beautiful thing I've ever seen.

Finally, he removes my bindings and slides his arms beneath me, hoisting me up and onto his lap. "Ride me, Vanessa, ride me hard."

I strap my legs around him and begin to move, rocking forward and back, wrapping my arms around his neck. He grasps my ass to help me get more leverage, and his breaths become harsh gasps. "Can't—wait—any longer."

He flips me onto my back and starts fucking me with abandon, grunting and pumping his hips wildly. When he grits his teeth, I know he's about to come—and I'm about to do it again. I jump off that cliff first, my body bowing up and my nails biting into his back.

Craig lets out a primal roar as he comes. With two more thrusts, he's done. Then he pulls out of my body and lies down beside me, breathing too hard to speak. So instead, he aims a sloppy grin at me.

I'm breathless too, so I reciprocate the sloppiness.

Who knew divorced sex could be this incredible?

Chapter Twenty

Craig

Last night. What can I say about it? Nothing that wouldn't sound moronic. Vanessa and I bonded in the most surprising ways last night, thanks to Holly's little bag of goodies. Vanessa and I had intended to try more new positions, with and without bondage, but we were too tired after the first time. Yeah, we are not teenagers anymore. We middle-aged people need a nice long break between athletic sexual encounters.

So yes, we fell asleep after wolfing down our desserts. Vanessa didn't tell me to go back to my bungalow. She cuddled up under the covers with me and draped one arm and one leg over me too. I keep needing to remind myself that wanting to cuddle doesn't mean she wants to marry me again. My mind—okay, it might actually be my heart—insists on encouraging me to believe that is what is means. I love her even more now than I did when we got married all those years ago.

But I need to take it slow. Really slow. If I rush, Vanessa might run away.

I roll my head to the side, gazing at the face of the only woman I've ever loved. She looks peaceful and sweet, younger too, as if sleep had stripped away all her anxiety and annoyance. I brush a few stray hairs away from her eyes, and that old pang hits me in the chest again.

She moans softly and wriggles against me. Then her lids flutter open. She smiles in the sweetest way. "Good morning, Craig."

"Good morning, Nessa. What should we do today?"

"Let's have sex again and figure out the rest after."

I can't help chuckling. "You've turned into a nymphomaniac, haven't you?"

She kicks my leg. "If I am, so are you."

"What should we do about that?"

"Already told you. We will fuck again."

The way she said that so matter-of-factly makes me want to hug her. I settle for kissing her forehead. "Plain vanilla or spicy?"

"What do you think?"

"Spicy it is. I had an idea last night that we didn't get around to trying." I wince. "But I can't remember what it was now."

"Ah, the vagaries of age. Why don't we go out on the patio and see what happens?"

"I love your new spontaneity."

She smiles and pushes up onto her elbow, then kisses me. "I need to pee first. Go on out to the patio, and I'll meet you there."

"Perfect."

She hops off the bed and glances back at me over her shoulder.

I turn onto my side and watch her sexy ass while she heads for the bathroom. But she closes the door, cutting off my view. Sighing, I slide off the bed and amble out onto the private patio. A temperate breeze wafts over me, bringing with it the scent of flowers, though I can't tell where that aroma originated. The resort has flowering trees and bushes, so maybe there's one of those right below the patio. A smattering of puffy little clouds wander across the deep blue sky.

Life couldn't get any better than this.

"Enjoying the scenery?"

I turn to look at Vanessa. "Scenery isn't what I'm enjoying right now. Your beautiful body has captured all my attention."

She had been holding her hands behind her back, but now she moves them in front of her to reveal the two lollipops she's holding. "We never did get around to sucking on these little goodies."

"Are those the red wine lollipops? It's kind of early for alcohol."

"We aren't guzzling a whole bottle." She offers me a lollipop. "Think of it as an appetizer before we feast on each other."

I grab the candy on a stick, then freeze. Why? Because Vanessa just slipped her lollipop between her lips and puckered them. Her cheeks cave in a little as she sucks on the hard candy. Then she slides it out millimeter by millimeter. "Mm, this tastes almost as good as you. Go on, suck on it, Craig."

The husky tone of her voice ensures that I will do anything she says. I set the round red disk on my tongue and close my lips over it, suckling the candy. I groan, but not because the lollipop tastes good, though it does. I groan because Vanessa just raked her tongue over her lollipop and curled it around the candy. When she slides it into her mouth again, thrusting it in and out, over and over, I almost choke on my own tongue.

I wind up coughing instead.

She drops her lollipop. "Craig, are you okay? Maybe I should do the Heimlich maneuver."

"No, I'm fine, I swear." I pick up her lollipop and set it on the patio table along with mine. "These things are dangerous. Better stick to eating you up."

"Well, if you really are recovered..."

"I am. Completely."

"Then where should we do it? On the chaise, on the table, against the railing..."

She slides her arms around my waist, pressing her body to mine. "Why don't you surprise me?"

Just a few days ago, I would've been shocked if she said that to me. Vanessa had never liked being caught off guard. But everything has changed.

I splay my palm over her upper back, push my other hand into her hair, and kiss her. We take it slow, savoring every movement and every flavor, drunk on each other more than those lollipops could ever intoxicate us. Even wine couldn't outdo this feeling.

When we finally give up each other's lips, I'm halfway to an erection.

Vanessa's mouth forms a lazy, satisfied smile. "I've changed my mind. Let's not have sex, not right now."

"I wish you'd told me that before I kissed you that way. I'm on the verge of a hard-on already."

"Are you really disappointed? Because I was thinking we could go to the waterfall and swim."

I touch my forehead to hers. "When I'm with you, I'm never disappointed."

"Then you want to go swimming?"

"Yes. And let's take a picnic breakfast with us."

She smiles again, but this time it's bright and full of joy. I swear that expression could light up the whole world. She folds her arms around my neck, and her lips graze my ear. "I think fate brought us to this island, and I'm so glad it did."

Fate? I guess that's my new first name. I should tell her the truth about how we both wound up at this resort. But then she kisses me and smiles, and I get instant amnesia. I will tell her. Later. I have less than two weeks to confess, but that means I don't need to do it today.

Just a few more days, that's all I need. A few more days before I drop that bomb on her.

Or maybe a week more.

We take a shower together, soaping each other up and splashing each other. It's like we've traveled back in time to the early days of our marriage, when we loved to have fun and couldn't get enough of each other. Vanessa calls room service to order a picnic breakfast for us. We wait in the lobby for Emilio to bring us our food, which comes in an actual basket. We thank him and head out to the waterfall.

As we approach the area, the sound of the water grows louder and louder, though it's never deafening. The spray generates a full rainbow, like the one we'd seen while zip-lining. Is that a sign? I've never believed in that bullshit, but I can't help feeling like the universe is trying to tell me something. *Stop lying to Vanessa,* that's probably what the universe wants me to do.

Just a few more days. I swear I'll confess then.

If I think the words "a few more days" again, they won't even sound like words anymore.

We amble over the bridge and find a nice little spot near the waterfall where we can enjoy our picnic. I gaze up at the sky, wondering again how it can be so deep blue, untainted by any kind of pollution, not even contrails from airliners. The pristine skies only add to the mystique of this place, which has begun to feel like an alternate reality to me. Vanessa doesn't hate me. We're both naked twenty-four seven. We went zip-lining. That's definitely some sort of alternate universe.

Just as we finish our meal, I glance at Vanessa and see something that robs me of breath. She sits there smiling at me, her eyes sparkling, with the spray from the waterfall misting up behind her and casting a faint, shimmering rainbow. I've never seen anything more beautiful in my life, and I'm not talking about the rainbow. How could I ever have walked away from this woman?

I can't resist reaching out to trail my fingers down her cheek.

She grasps my hand, turning it flat so she can kiss the palm. Her sweet smile makes my throat tighten. "Let's jump into the waterfall pool and swim around."

"Love to."

We dive into the waterfall pool. It feels comfortably cool, and when we tip our heads back, we get a stunning view of the forest canopy and the sky. A bright yellow bird flies by, above the spray from the falls. Vanessa grins and laughs when she sees the bird, and I get that pang in my chest again. I love her, but I won't tell her that again. I've said it at least twice since we came to this island, so she knows how I feel.

As we paddle around in the pool, I notice there seems to be a shadowed area behind the falls. Could there be a cave behind the curtain of water? Nothing in the information I have about the resort mentions anything like that.

"Hey, Vanessa!" I call out, trying to get her attention. She's been infatuated with a clump of flowers that hangs over the edge, almost touching the water. When she turns to look at me, I shout, "Come over here! Think I found something."

She swims over to me. "What is it?"

I point to the thundering cascade. "Does it seem to you like there might be a cavern or something behind the waterfall?"

Vanessa holds her hand up like a visor and squints at the shadows behind the waterfall. "You know what, I think there just might be a cavern back there. Wanna check it out?"

"Absolutely." I wave toward the falls. "Ladies first? Or would you rather send me in to make sure there aren't any bears hiding back there?"

"This island doesn't have bears."

"Snakes, then."

Vanessa wrinkles her nose. "Good point. You can go first."

"What happened to woman power?"

"The woman code has a clause that states men will go first into potentially snake-infested areas."

"Is that so."

I slap her ass under the water, which is surprisingly difficult to do. Then I swim to the edge of the falls, where there's a gap behind the curtain of water. This does look like a ledge. I set my hands on it and push up, hoisting myself onto the mostly flat area. Mist from the waterfall billows around me, and the rumble of the falls is louder back here, of course. Vanessa would give me an exasperated look if she heard me say that. If we were in our twenties, she'd tell me "duh."

Actually, I think she did say that to me back when we were in college. I was a computer geek in training, and she was the sexy biology major. And yeah, I'm pretty sure she used to employ the "duh" word every time I said something goofy.

Vanessa swims up to the edge of the falls, right beside the cascade. Her lips move, but I can't hear what she said.

I cup my hand over my ear and shake my head.

She hoists that beautiful body up and onto the ledge, then jogs over to me. "Is it safe? I don't see any snakes."

"Seems pretty safe to me."

I clasp her hand as we move closer to the rock wall and tiptoe along it, searching for...who knows what. Maybe this is a forbidden zone, off limits to guests, but nothing in the welcome packet mentioned anything like that. Halfway across the ledge, I pause to study a darker area that seems like a fissure in the rock wall. Vanessa leans around me to peer into that spot too. I hold up a hand in the universal gesture for "don't move."

She nods.

I release her hand so I can feel around inside the fissure. It's much wider than I had realized and clearly doesn't go more than six feet up, nowhere near as high as the cliff itself. The waterfall acts like a sort of sunshade, turning this hidden ledge into a twilight world all its own. Vines have grown inside the fissure, and thanks to my cautious feeling-around, I can now tell the vegetation has hidden just how wide and deep this fissure is.

But I need confirmation from a science expert. So, I twist around to speak directly into Vanessa's ear. "Mind taking a look at this fissure? I'd love your opinion on whether it's bigger than it seems."

She nods, then moves to the other side of me and shoos me away.

I back up a few feet, just enough to give her room to work. She makes the cutest face of intense concentration as she explores the fissure, scrunching up her features while her tongue pokes out between her teeth. I'm glad no one could hear my thoughts. "Scrunching" is a term our daughter April loves to use. It's contagious, apparently.

Vanessa's eyes flare wide briefly, then she smiles with satisfaction.

I shuffle closer. "It's more than a fissure, isn't it?"

"Oh, yes. It's much more than that." She starts tugging on the vines, apparently to clear the way. "We need a knife or a machete to get this gunk out of the way."

"No, we don't." I shoo her away. "I've been working out, remember?"

She crosses her arms over her chest and observes while I grasp a handful of vines and yank. Then I yank again. I can feel the vines are loosening up, so I keep going, pulling and pulling and pulling while the vegetation gradually gives way. I wrench a lump free and toss the vines over my shoulder. Now I can see that I don't need to clear the whole width of the fissure. I only need to rip out the parts closest t the opening. The space gets wider beyond that.

I wrench a few more lumps out of the fissure and throw them away, then I dust off my palms and nod toward the fissure. "See? No machete required."

Her eyes widen. Her jaw drops. She blinks quickly several times.

Then Vanessa grasps my head and plants a big, wet kiss on me. "That was amazing. Like something out of an Indiana Jones movie."

"Let's just hope there isn't a giant stone ball waiting in there to crush us."

"I'm sure you could push it out of the way if there was one." She peers into the crevice. "Should we go in there?"

"Why not? We both came to this island for adventure and excitement."

And there's no one else I'd rather go on an adventure with than Vanessa.

Chapter Twenty-One

Vanessa

Ignaw on my bottom lip, studying the seemingly narrow opening in the rock wall. It might be bigger than it seems, or it might get even tighter. What if we get stuck in there? I don't have my phone with me, and I doubt Craig has his. Well, it's time to take another risk. Zip-lining worked out, so exploring this fissure might too. So, I turn to Craig. "Who should go first? I don't think it's wide enough for us to walk in side by side."

"Oh, I think it is—once we get past this narrower part. So the question is, do you trust me?"

I clasp his hand. "Absolutely I do. But maybe you should go first, in case there are snakes."

"You and Indiana Jones have a lot in common, don't you? He didn't like snakes either."

"Ha-ha. The man who shrieks when he sees a spider shouldn't harass me."

Craig taps my nose with one finger. "I have never shrieked. You must be confusing me with someone else."

I love that we're teasing each other again, like we used to do when we were married. It feels...right.

Craig keeps hold of my hand while he shimmies through the narrow section with me right behind him. It's dark in here, but I can see light up ahead, and the fissure seems to be veering to the left. We're only a few yards in when the fissure opens up into a much wider crevice that could accommodate at least four people standing side by side. Craig and I study our surroundings, and I can tell he's as amazed by this hidden treasure as I am. No, we didn't find any actual treasure. But this little hideaway is incredible.

Brightly colored flowers emerge from the ground and from small holes in the crevice walls. We can now see that the vines Craig had torn out to make a path for us are attached to trees high above us—on top of the cliff, I'd bet. Their roots poke out in some spots. A dark brown butterfly swoops down low over our heads, and I get a glimpse of the critter's bright blue and white spots.

I can't help it. I get so excited when I see that little beastie, so I grin and shout, "Oh, look! Did you see that blue moon butterfly? I read about that one."

"When did you read about butterflies?"

"I bought books about the wildlife on this island, and it included butterflies as well as birds."

"Snakes too? No, you would've shrieked when you saw a picture of one of those."

He smirked when he said that. Craig is having too much fun harassing me, but I don't mind at all. I'm sure I'll find ways to harass him right back.

We continue through the wide crevice and see various kinds of plants, though neither of us knows what they're called. I hadn't read about flora, only the fauna. As we stop to admire the large blooms of a plant that has grown out of a hole in the crevice, I spot something incredible and yelp.

"Look at that, Craig! It's a crimson shining parrot."

"A what? I don't see anything."

I hook a finger under his chin and lift. "Look up. It landed on that big tree root."

Craig tips his head back and squints. "That thing? What's special about it? I think my grandmother had one of those."

"I doubt that very much. The species is endemic to Fiji and Heirani Motu."

I gaze up at the beautiful creature, with its green and blue wings and red body. The colors are so bright and gorgeous, and the parrot's eyes are a striking shade of gold.

Craig gazes up at the parrot too and seems to appreciate it more the longer he admires the creature. "What does 'endemic' mean?"

"It means the species is native to those geographic locations."

"Well, I can't deny that little guy is pretty."

"A minute ago, you said it's nothing special."

He smirks at me. "I was teasing you, Nessa. Can't resist doing that. You're sexy when you get annoyed."

Craig leads the way as we travel deeper into the crevice, going far enough that we can't hear the rumbling of the waterfall anymore. The songs of birds and the rustling of the trees fill the silence left behind by the thundering cascade, and we continue holding hands as we explore this hidden world.

Finally, we emerge into a small cove.

"Where are we?" I ask, though it's a rhetorical question.

But Craig answers anyway. "We might be on the other side of the island. Everything we've seen before today was on the side that houses the resort. This must be the empty backside."

"Are you sure it's empty?"

"Don't worry. I'll watch out for snakes, and you can jump on my back if you spot one."

I lodge my hands on my hips. "You are the king of exaggeration, aren't you? I don't shriek when I see a snake, and I would not leap on your back because of that."

"Are you sure?"

"Yes."

"Hmm." He points at the ground behind me. "Then that shouldn't bother you at all."

"What shouldn't bother me?"

His lips twitch, as if he's trying not to smirk. "The snake that's slithering toward you."

I shriek and leap onto his back. Only then do I realize there's nothing on the ground except grass. I slide off his back and smack his arm. "You rat."

Craig laughs. "That was a rotten thing to do. Sorry. But I couldn't resist. You were so adamant that snakes don't scare you."

"You know what this means." I lift myself up onto my toes to speak directly into his ear. "I will find a way to get back at you."

"Go on. I can handle it."

"We're acting like children, aren't we?"

He shrugs. "Maybe that's what we need to do right now. We spent most of our lives taking care of the kids. Now, it's our turn to go wild."

Maybe he's right about that. Sometimes I feel like an idiot, the way I've been behaving since I came to this island. But other times, I'm sure this is exactly what I've needed for a long, long time. Heirani Motu has changed my life.

Craig reclaims my hand, leading me out into the little cove.

We wander through the palm trees and past mangroves, casually swinging our joined hands while we admire the magical atmosphere that this island has woven around us. Craig spots a coconut tree and releases my hand to rush over there. I hurry after him.

He slaps his palm on the tree's trunk. "How about a little coconut milk to refresh you?"

"The coconuts are way up there." I point straight up. "Don't think it's a wise plan to climb that high."

"Who said I was going to climb up there? I'll shake it down."

"That won't work."

He slaps the trunk again, then plants both palms on its surface and begins to push. Nothing happens, naturally. He pushes harder. Still nothing. The leaves don't even shiver.

"Give it up, He-Man. You can't get a coconut that way."

He flattens his lips and studies the tree, with his hands on his hips. I can hear him clucking his tongue, something he often does while he's working out a problem. At last, he gives up and steps away from the tree.

Then he runs at it full speed and leaps up.

And he falls right back down.

"I told you, Craig, you won't get a coconut out of that tree. It's at least thirty feet tall."

He bows his head, hands on his hips, and sighs. After a moment, he marches over to me. "I surrender. No coconuts for us today. Let's go look at that red tree instead."

"I doubt you can get a coconut from that one. I saw a picture of a tree like that in the welcome packet, and it was called a flame tree."

"Fascinating." He surveys our surroundings. "Maybe we should go back to the waterfall. Don't want to get lost out here."

"Sounds like an excellent idea. We don't want to become the subjects of a massive manhunt."

I'm just grateful that he gave up on trying to shake a coconut out of a tree. What on earth got into him today? I don't care if he can achieve silly feats of machismo. That's not why I married him in the first place, and it certainly wouldn't be a reason for me to tie the knot with him again.

Am I considering that idea? Not sure.

By the time we reach the waterfall, I'm already starting to feel hungry. We had walked quite a distance. That must have used up a lot of calories. We've just squeezed through the narrowest part of the hidden passage and emerged into the space behind the thundering cascade.

Craig turns toward me.

His expression tells me everything I need to know. He wants to kiss me. Maybe he wants more than that too. My pulse speeds up, and a tingle of excitement sweeps over me from head to toe. My breaths have grown shallower, as if I can't pull in enough oxygen because the anticipation has left me breathless. I do feel that way. The thrill of what will come next has transfixed me.

Craig slides his arms around my waist and tugs me close. Our bodies meet just as he seals his lips over mine.

How can this be so exciting? I've kissed him countless times in the past, yet the feel of his lips pressed to mine, here in this moment, feels as electrifying as the very first time we kissed. My lids close. My body slackens. We revel in the sensual delight of tasting and teasing each other, and when he slides one hand down to my bottom, I know I'm lost.

After a few minutes of kissing, we peel our bodies away from each other and hurry out from under the waterfall to leap into the pool. That's the only way to get back on dry land. Craig hoists himself up and onto the bank, then grasps my hands to help me up. We're drenched again, but neither of us cares. Hand in hand, we make our way back to the resort proper. The clock above the front desk tells us we spent about two hours exploring the hidden wonders behind the waterfall.

It didn't feel like that long. I could've spent days in that secret sanctuary with Craig, and I wouldn't have minded at all. In fact, I might love to live there with him. The thought stops me, but only for a moment. Yes, I might want to live with him, anywhere in the world.

"Are you okay, Vanessa?"

I look at Craig and smile. "I've never felt better."

"Neither have I. What should we do until dinner?"

That simple question shouldn't turn me on, but it does. I'm getting some naughty ideas. "Care to join me in my suite? I still have that bag of goodies."

He leans closer to whisper, "Do you mean the paper bag Holly gave us?"

"Mm-hm."

"What are we waiting for?" He claims my hand as he starts hustling down the corridor. "I can't refuse an offer like that. It's harder to turn down than a mafia deal."

Once we get inside my room, I tell him to lie on the bed and keep his eyes closed. Beyond the patio, I can hear guests laughing and water splashing, but none of that matters. I have one goal, and I will implement it. Craig doesn't even try to peek, as far as I can tell, but I knew he wouldn't. He loved our games the other night as much as I did.

I suppose I should have realized how I really feel about him after that night in my suite. The next day, I had started to plan other games we could play. The thought of that excited me, but not only in a sexual way. I felt excitement at the prospect of spending more time with him. Will having dirty fun together save our broken marriage? I don't know. And for now, I won't worry about that.

Ever since that hot night in my suite, I've been making plans. And Craig is about to find out what I've concocted.

I start to head for the bathroom.

"Where are you going, Vanessa?"

Spinning around, I wag a finger at him. "You naughty boy. I told you to stay put and keep your eyes closed."

"Couldn't help it. How can I resist the chance to see your sexy ass in motion? A man only has so much willpower."

"Hmm. I guess I'll need to take more drastic measures to protect the integrity of my surprise for you." I return to the bed and dig around in the bag of goodies until I find what I need. Then I raise the blindfold. "Are you okay with this?"

"Anything you want."

I tie the blindfold around his head, then realize he still has his hands free. Can I trust him not to lift the blindfold and peek? Of course I can't. He wants to ogle my ass. So, I excavate another item from the goody bag. "Think I'd better restrain you, to make sure you can't peek."

"Go on, I don't mind."

I secure his wrists with the lavender-padded handcuffs, hooking them through one of the headboard slats. "There. Now I'm going into the bathroom for a few minutes."

"Don't take too long. Just thinking about what you're up to is getting me hard. I might go off without you."

"You can handle the suspense. I have faith in you."

Only once I reach the bathroom do I realize what I said. *I have faith in you.* That might have been an offhanded comment, but I meant it. We might have lost our way for a while, but we've both regained our faith in each other and our relationship.

I waltz back into the bedroom area, where the sun beams in through the glass doors of the patio. That's not quite the mood I'm looking for, so I pull the patio curtains shut. That creates a whisking sound that makes Craig perk up. He lifts his head, but he can't remove the blindfold to see what I'm doing. The resort's welcome packet had mentioned that every suite and bungalow includes blackout curtains for guests who have trouble sleeping when the daylight lasts so long during certain times of the year. The curtains create a twilight atmosphere, while the lamp on the nightstand adds just enough extra glow to make this a sensual atmosphere.

As I walk toward the bed, my costume makes a jingling sound. While I had pulled the curtains shut, I doubt Craig had noticed that faint tinkling. Now, he lifts his head again, clearly curious, though he refrains from speaking.

I lean over the bed, ready to remove his blindfold, but I hesitate. "Can I trust you to keep your eyes closed briefly? Just until I get in position."

"You can trust me."

I remove the blindfold, which leaves him still handcuffed to the headboard. He sticks to his word and does not open his eyes. I back away from the bed, finding the best viewing spot.

"Open your eyes, Craig, and tell me what you think."

His lids flutter open, and he stares at me. His tongue slips out to moisten his lips. "I didn't think you could rock my world any more than you already have this week. But damn, Vanessa, you did it again."

Chapter Twenty-Two

Craig

I must be hallucinating. My ex-wife can't really be standing there in a skimpy belly dancer outfit, wearing smoky eye makeup and red lipstick, seeming like she intends to have her way with me while I lie here handcuffed to the bed. Vanessa never did anything like this until we came to Heirani Motu. Something about this island has changed us both, or maybe it just freed us to try new things. Either way, I can't wait to see what Vanessa does next.

"Are you going to dance for me, Nessa?"

She drags one finger down her chest, between her tits, and nods slowly.

"Will this be a ventriloquist routine?"

Vanessa shakes her head.

"Are you planning to say nothing for all of whatever you plan on doing to me? Or for me?"

She nods again.

Well, okay. I'll just lie here and let her do her thing.

The skirt she's wearing has two halves, one that hangs down in front and another that hangs over her ass. A sequined strap holds the skirt up and reveals the sides of her hips. She's barefoot too, and she teased her hair in the sexiest way. The bra-like top barely covers those luscious breasts and features more sequins.

"You're going to belly dance, right?"

She nods.

Oddly, her refusal to speak makes me even more turned on. Dirty talk is hot, but her silence might just drive me insane in the best way.

Vanessa leans over at the foot of the bed and picks up a small portable radio, not quite a boombox, but big enough to accommodate a CD. We're showing our age now for sure. Nobody uses a portable CD player anymore. Do they? Our youngest daughter thinks anything that doesn't come with earbuds is completely old-fashioned and passé. April will find out eventually that everyone becomes an old-fashioned weirdo sooner or later.

My ex-wife sets the CD player on a chair at the foot of the bed, then switches it on. Belly dancer type music emanates from the small speakers, though they have surprisingly good sound for their size. Vanessa raises her arms and rolls her wrists to make her bracelets jangle. Then she bends one knee, keeping her toes on the floor, and begins to shake her hips in that way belly dancers do, dropping one hip repeatedly while she keeps her toes on the floor.

The swift movements make her breasts jiggle, and I'm going cross-eyed trying to watch her hips and her tits at the same time, incapable of choosing one or the other. How could any man choose? She has the most beautiful body in the world.

Vanessa sets her raised foot down and gives up on popping her hips. She stands still for a few seconds, then holds her arms waist height, elbows tucked, and begins to undulate her belly like a sensual cobra rising from its basket. I observe in rapt fascination while she holds her arms out to the side and turns in a slow circle while still undulating. I can't tear my gaze away from her belly and the little white jewel tucked into her navel. She has clearly timed her dancing to the music on the CD player, because when she started to undulate, the beat became deeper and attuned to her movements.

Do I have a hard-on now? I must be halfway there for sure, but I can't do a visual inspection of my dick right now, not when she's dancing for me.

She starts to lift her feet and set them down again, delicately, slowly, in rhythm with the music. Then she gives up undulating and instead swirls her hips while lifting and dropping them too. The motion seems almost like a figure eight, but I don't give a fuck about the pattern, not when she's dragging her finger down her breastbone and biting her lip. I'm struggling to catch my breath, and I know I've got a rock-hard erection now.

Vanessa tips her back just enough to give me a good look at the sensual curve of her throat. She spreads her legs a bit and lowers herself toward the floor inch by inch, in no hurry to finish her dance routine. She keeps on swiveling her hips and now undulates her shoulders too. Her lips have fallen open. She traces the tip of her tongue over her upper teeth.

I try to speak but only manage to splutter.

The front half of her skirt hangs down between her legs, and she skates her palms up and down her exposed thighs, taking her time, and never looking away from me. When she grasps her knees and pushes them wider apart, I get a glimpse of the hairs on her mound.

My chest is heaving. My cock feels like an iron rod.

"Remove the cuffs, Nessa. I need to get my hands on you right now."

She shakes her head, then drops to her knees and bends over backward to undulate some more.

"I'll have a stroke if you don't stop torturing me." Not that I mind this kind of torture, but I don't want to come all over the bed without even touching her.

She lowers all of her body onto the floor and lays there for a minute while the CD winds down. Her tits are heaving, just like my chest. Finally, she rolls onto her side and gets up, shuffling over to the bed, where she perches on the edge. "Want me to fuck you now?"

"Yes, baby, right now."

She reaches behind her back to unhook the sequined bra and toss it onto the floor.

I might be drooling. Her tits unleashed are breathtaking.

Vanessa hops off the bed just long enough to push the skirt over her hips and let it drop to the floor. Then she climbs onto the mattress and straddles my lap. For a moment, she sits there gazing down at me without saying a word. I'm about to open my mouth when she beats me to it.

"Time to ride the cobra, Craig."

"You're the cobra. The way you danced proved it."

She rakes her nails lightly down my chest. "I summoned the snake, but your cock is the serpent I'm going to ride."

Vanessa slants toward me and drags her tongue over my lips. Then she sits up and rises to her knees, grasping my cock to position it perfectly. I need to touch her, but she won't let me. My handcuffs thump as I unconsciously tug on them in my desperation to lay my hands on her.

With her hand wrapped around my erection, she gradually lowers herself onto my body until I'm snugly sheathed by her hot, slick flesh. A groan resonates in my chest. She feels so fucking good, and I love the look on her face, full of hunger and sweetness, which seems like a contradiction. Only she can merge those two expressions.

Vanessa leans forward to open my handcuffs and toss them away.

She begins to rock, taking her time, relishing the sensations as much as I am. The feel of her silky flesh wrapped around my dick might be the most perfect sensation I've ever experienced. She sets her hands on my chest and lifts herself off my cock just a little with every forward motion. I grasp her waist but don't try to take over, letting her set the pace and the heat level, reveling in the beauty of her body and the passion that shows on her face and in the sounds she makes.

I lunge my head up and try to catch one of her nipples with my mouth, but she sits up again, robbing me of the taste of her nipple. I bend my knees to frame her body with them.

She slaps my knees. "Legs flat."

"Yes, ma'am."

I straighten my legs, and she moves her knees forward so she can set her feet flat on the bed, straddling me. Then she leans backward to set her hands on my ankles. With her arms straight, she throws her head back and resumes riding me. Her new position lifts her tits. I can't stop staring at those globes as they jiggle with every move she makes, and I instinctively grasp her knees while she rocks her hips in a slow rhythm that drives me crazy. I want to drive into her hard and fast, but I can't do anything. The vision of her in this new pose has mesmerized me.

Vanessa gets more excited as sharp cries erupt out of her. The way she rides me becomes more excited too, and she bounces her body up and down my cock so wildly that I can hear the sucking sound her sheath creates with every lunge. It makes her tits bounce wildly. The bed thumps. She chants "yes, yes, yes" while the bedsprings creak and her cries grow louder and more impassioned.

I'm breathing so hard I couldn't shout even if I wanted to do it. Grunts and groans are all I can manage. My cock feels like it might explode if I don't come right now, so I thrust a hand out to rub her clit.

She freezes with her body slanted backward. Her nails dig into my ankles. Her head snaps forward, and she lets out a wild, throaty cry as her body clenches me over and over. I grab the headboard rails to get enough leverage, then thrust my hips upward, coming so hard that I grit my teeth and my knuckles ache from gripping the headboard.

Once I'm done, Vanessa rolls off my body and snuggles up to my side. For a few minutes, we simply lie here recovering from the earth-shattering climaxes we both experienced. Are middle-aged people supposed to have sex like that? I'd assumed that once I got into my fifties, everything would start to gradually slide downhill in the sex department. But since we came to this island, I've discovered that age isn't a life sentence of walkers and Viagra. Even senior citizens get wild and crazy here.

I honestly think this island must have magical powers.

Don't think I'll tell Vanessa that. Sounding like a lunatic won't convince her to come back to me.

She drapes an arm over my chest, twirling her finger around my nipple. "I guess you enjoyed my belly dancing."

"I didn't just enjoy it. I loved it. Watching you dance got me so hot for you that I'm pretty sure my brain melted."

"And you liked the new position too?"

"Holy shit, Nessa." I roll over to face her, our noses almost touching. "I more than liked that position. I loved it so much that I saw stars when I came."

She grins. "My heart was pounding so hard that I couldn't breathe. Holly's little book of sex positions did wonders for us."

"Yeah, that's putting it mildly."

Vanessa glances away for a moment, then meets my gaze while tapping one finger on my lips. "I love you, Craig. I want us to be a couple again, forever this time."

"I want that too. I love you so much, Vanessa, and I'm sorry I walked away from our marriage. That will never happen again."

She presses her lips to mine. "I know you won't run away again. Neither of us will."

The sweetest smile curves her lips.

And that expression gives me a hard pang in my chest. I need to tell her the truth, right now, tonight, no matter what happens after that.

I force myself to look into her eyes. "I need to tell you something, Vanessa. It will sound horrible, and I won't blame you if you smack me and march out the door once you know the truth."

"Spit it out, Craig."

"Remember that letter you got in the mail? The one that said you'd won a free two-week stay at this resort?"

"Of course I remember. So what?"

A lump forms in my throat, but I clear my throat and keep going. "I sent that letter."

She stares at me, not blinking, frozen with her gaze nailed to mine. "I don't understand. You forwarded that letter?"

"No. I wrote it. You didn't win a free vacation, because I paid for all of it and made the travel arrangements."

"Why would you do that?" The confusion in her voice and on her face sends a chill rushing through me. "Are you saying you tricked me into coming here?"

"Yes."

"Because...you wanted me back?"

"Yes."

She remains perfectly still, though her lids blink slowly now. Her lips have fallen open. Vanessa sits up, her forehead wrinkled.

"Are you okay?" I ask. "Please say something. Punch me, kick me, spit on me, scream obscenities. But don't just sit there like a statue. I can explain—"

"No." She clambers off me to hop off the bed, but then sits there with her legs dangling. "Tell me why you did this. Tell me everything."

She hates me, doesn't she? But I need to explain right now.

Chapter Twenty-Three

Vanessa

Maybe I've fallen asleep, and this is some kind of nightmare. But no, this is not a dream. Craig just confessed that he tricked me into coming to this island as part of a plot to get me back. I still don't understand any of this, and I'm waiting for him to explain. He brought me to a nudist island because he thought that would convince me to marry him again? That makes no sense.

How do I feel? He won't find that out until after he confesses everything.

Okay, I just told him I love him a few minutes ago, so he knows how I feel. My mind is reeling from this revelation, and I'm not thinking clearly. Besides, I might change my mind about loving him depending on what he says next.

But God, I do love him. Always have, always will.

He sits up, though he doesn't move to perch on the bed's edge beside me. "You want to know exactly what I did. The answer is that I made all the travel reservations, and I chose this resort because it's not like any place we've ever visited before. I needed to get you alone, so we could talk. You had stopped responding to my phone calls and texts."

"That was childish. I'm sorry. But we stopped communicating, and I couldn't think of another way to get your attention." I cover my face with my hands and moan pitifully. Then I turn my body toward him. "It was a stupid idea. But I had convinced myself that the way to solve our problems was to give you a big shock."

"Like moving out."

"And later, ignoring your calls and texts. Neither of us handled the empty-nest period very well."

"No, we didn't. You moved out, and I filed for divorce. What kind of idiots are we?"

I laugh, though it's not a cheerful sound. "The kind who are blind, stubborn, and clueless."

He slides onto the bed's edge beside me. "Do you regret coming to Heirani Motu?"

"No. I've come alive again, even more than I was when we first got married. I feel...reinvigorated."

His expression tightens into a near grimace. "And, ah, how do you feel about me and what I did?"

I take a moment to consider everything that's happened. "I'm not angry. Maybe I should be, but the time I've spent here has helped me look back at the past with a clearer gaze. Our downfall began on the day when Greg left for college. Then a few years later, Nicole went off to college too. And a few years after that, April was gone. We had a lot of changes to deal with, but instead of doing that, we buried our heads in the sand."

"You still haven't told me how you feel, knowing what I did to get your here."

"If you had asked me on the first day, I would have jumped on the next flight back to America. Learning the truth now has changed things." I clasp his hand. "I love you, Craig, and I want to spend the rest of our time here figuring out where we go next."

"How does that process begin?"

"It already has. Let's treat this like a vacation—but one with real communication and total honesty."

He smiles. "Sounds like a plan."

And this is the moment when everything changes.

We take a shower together, then head for the front desk to ask if we can share my suite and give up Craig's bungalow. The answer is yes. We are now cohabitating. Living in sin, as our parents would have called it. These days, it's just the trendy thing to do. As we head out of the resort, we halt on the main patio and look at each other at the same time. I know we're thinking the same thing too.

Still, I feel like I should say the words. We aren't telepathic, after all, so maybe I don't really know what he thinks. "Should we tell James and Holly about the hidden passage behind the waterfall?"

"Definitely."

We return to the front desk and let the clerk know we need to speak to the big bosses. The nice young man snatches up the phone and calls James and Holly. Just a few minutes later, the couple walks into the lobby.

"You wanted to speak with us?" James says. "Are you wanting to plan a wedding?"

Holly elbows him in the side. "Let them tell us what they need. Don't try to read their minds."

"Sorry." He clears his throat and starts again. "What can we do for you?"

I glance at Craig, but he shrugs. I assume that means he wants me to explain. "Yesterday, we walked down to the waterfall and got curious about what's behind it."

"There's a ledge."

"Yes. But we got even more curious and made a discovery. There's a hidden passage in the rock wall. It had been filled in with vegetation, but we managed to clear enough of it to go into the passage and out the other side."

Holly's brows shoot up. "Out the other side? This sounds like a fantastic mystery."

"Would you like to come with us and see the passage for yourself?"

"Yes, yes, yes!" She claps her hands. "I love a good mystery."

James rolls his eyes at Holly, but he's smiling too. "Try to restrain your enthusiasm somewhat, darling. We haven't seen this hidden passage yet."

I suddenly realize they aren't wearing their work uniforms. "Are you guys off duty today?"

"Yes, we are," James replies. "That means we can accompany you to the waterfall. But first, we will need to dress appropriately."

He looks at Holly, and she nods.

Then they both strip naked.

I cover my mouth to squelch the laughter that wants to burst out of me. I wind up spluttering instead. "That's what you meant by dressing appropriately?"

The general manager smirks. "Of course. We prefer to go nude when we're off the clock."

I guess that makes a strange kind of sense. They do run a nudist resort, after all. And I've heard rumors about how James and Holly get very, very naughty on their days off.

Craig and I lead the way, hand in hand, as we make our way along the main trail and turn down the waterfall path. James and Holly hold hands too. We chat and joke with each other along the way too. But once we reach the waterfall, all discussion stops. The only way to access the ledge is to leap into the water and then climb onto the ledge. It's too narrow for more than one person, so Craig jumps onto it first and offers me his hands to pull me up out of the water. James then hoists himself onto the ledge and assists his wife in getting up there too.

What a pair of gentlemen. Younger men aren't often like that these days.

Craig and I pad over to the hidden passage and glance inside it, just to be sure we hadn't hallucinated finding a secret world in there. Nope, we did not imagine it. A data scientist and a high school biology teacher actually stumbled onto a magical world on an island that was already magical, in my estimation. How else could I explain the way my relationship with Craig changed radically in less than a week?

We move aside, and Craig waves for James and Holly to come and see. Holly peeks into the passage first. She stays frozen for a moment, but then a brilliant grin lights up her face.

"James, you have to see this." She takes hold of his ear and drags him closer. "Look, it's amazing."

"Yes, it is quite nice."

She rolls her eyes. "Don't be so British about it. You're allowed to whoop and shout. This is an incredible discovery."

"Just wait," I say. "You haven't seen where the passage leads."

Holly steps back. "Show us, please. I can't wait. Maybe we'll find hidden treasure."

James gives his wife a patient smile. "Let's not go overboard from the start, pet."

Craig goes into the passage first, but I'm right behind him. We hold hands, of course, and James and Holly do the same as they follow us into the unknown. Craig and I know what lies inside and beyond this passage, but our friends have no idea. I feel a shiver of excitement as we make our way toward our destination, though I've seen what lies beyond this passage before. I shouldn't experience a thrill from going there again. What if, once we reach the secret cove, James and Holly announce that they've always known about it? Oh, who cares. I'm having the best vacation of my life either way, and it's all thanks to Craig.

The man I thought I never wanted to see again has opened my eyes in so many ways.

A banded iguana scuttles out from behind a rock and watches us as we stop to watch him. I know from my reading that males have wide bands of white and green while females are generally solid green. They have crested spines and very long toes. We all stand here for a moment admiring the beauty of this lizard with its long tail and stripes, the way he seems to pose for us with his head held high and then skitters away, out of our sight.

As we emerge from the passage, James and Holly seem genuinely awed by our surroundings. We're still walking through a narrow space, but now it's open to the air rather than covered by a natural roof. A crimson shining parrot swoops down from a tree high above our heads, and we all crane our necks to get a good look. The bird stops to roost on the root of a mangrove tree.

Holly grins and holds her hands in a prayer posture, touching them to her lips. I doubt she's actually praying, but she is genuinely thrilled. "I've never seen a parrot as beautiful as that one."

James tips his head back to gaze up at a flame tree that perches near the edge of the crevice. He seems awed by the tree, or maybe by the fact that it can thrive so close to the edge of a precipice.

When we leave the crevice and step out onto the beach, James and Holly both stop to gawk at the scenery. It is stunning, so I don't blame them. The beach here is sandy, but closer to the water, it becomes rockier. Smooth pebbles line the shore, so at least it's not sharp rocks or jagged slabs beneath the water.

James halts halfway to the rocky section of the beach and turns in a circle while shielding his eyes with his hand. "We saw this beach when the surveyors were here, trying to determine the best places to construct the main building and the outlying structures. This was before you came here, Holly. Eve and Val took me up in a helicopter to get a panoramic view."

"Who are Eve and Val?" Craig asks.

"The owners of the resort, Eve and Val Silva. They run the original Au Naturel Naturist Resort in Oregon."

"Is that a clothes-free resort too?"

"No. It's the family-friendly sort."

"You saw this beach from the air," I say. "But you've really never set foot on it before today?"

James shakes his head. "It was impossible to reach until you and Craig found the secret passage. Construction equipment couldn't be brought here, and that's why all the resort buildings are on the other side of the island."

"Will you announce the discovery of the passage and let guests explore this beach?"

"Not sure. We'll need to investigate all the legal and safety implications and whether or not the passage is natural or man-made. If humans created it, then there might be archaeological implications."

"That makes sense."

We explore the beach for a while longer, then return to the resort via the hidden passage. James and Holly ask us to keep the secret while they sort out the legalities, and we're more than happy to accommodate that request. Over the following several days, we enjoy everything the resort has to offer and get regular updates from James and Holly about the hidden passage. But it might take months or even years to sort out what the passage is and whether it's legal or safe to let guests wander around in there. For now, they have put up a barrier to prevent lookie-loos from wandering in there and a sign to explain that it's potentially dangerous.

Before I know it, our last day on Heirani Motu has arrived. In three hours, we will climb onto a plane and begin our journey home. James and Holly find us out on the main patio, sipping mojitos. They sit down at the table with us.

"We have some news," James tells us. "The beach you and Craig discovered now has a name. It's called Nessa's Cove."

"Is that a place name?" I ask. "Or someplace where you used to live?"

He chuckles. "No, pet. Nessa's Cove is named after you. Craig insisted on it."

My attention swerves to my ex-husband. "You asked James to name the cove after me?"

"Yes. It seemed appropriate. We found that secret passage together, but I would never have jumped up onto the waterfall ledge in the first place without you. I was trying to impress you. So it's appropriate that the beach is named after you."

I lean over and kiss him. "That's the sweetest thing you've ever done for me. Thank you."

The world now has a cove with my name on it. How strange. But I will never forget that Craig insisted on putting my name on that beach.

We chat with James and Holly for a bit longer, but then it's time to go. They accompany us out to the larger jet, where Rene is waiting to whisk us away to the Nausori International Airport in Suva. All the other passengers are already on board, but Craig stops us halfway to the jet.

"Do you mind if we do something first?" he asks James. "It'll only take a minute."

"Go on."

Craig roots around in his pants pocket and cups an object in his hand. I can't see what it is. Then he drops to one knee.

No, he can't be about to—That's crazy. We're too old for this.

He reveals the small box in his hand, flipping up the lid to show the diamond ring that lies nestled in satin. "Vanessa Angela Stendhal Hathaway, will you marry me again?"

"Middle-aged people don't get married."

"Of course they do." He holds the ring box higher. "I love you with everything I have, and I will keep on loving you and only you for the rest of my life and whatever comes after. So, Nessa, will you marry me again?"

Someone whoops. "Say yes, love, before the other passengers revolt."

Oh yes, that's Rene for sure.

I hold out my left hand. "Yes, Craig, of course I want to marry you. We've both made mistakes, but we found our way back to each other because of this magical island. All I want to do now is go home and begin our new life together."

He slides the ring onto my finger, sweeps me up in his arms, and kisses me.

Chapter Twenty-Four

Craig
Five weeks later

It still feels a little strange to be home again and not at a nudist resort where clothing is not allowed. Sometimes those two weeks on Heirani Motu seem like a strange and exciting dream, but I know it was real. I wouldn't be marrying the love of my life for the second time if it weren't for that island. James and Holly flew in for the big day. Introducing them to our kids didn't seem as weird as I'd expected.

Hey, come meet our nudist friends who love to have sex on a public beach. No, we didn't tell the kids that. Greg, Nicole, and April might be adults, but we have no desire to share the details of our vacation on an island populated with nudists.

While we waited for our second wedding day, I found a new job. James and Holly hired me as their data scientist, to help them market the resort more efficiently. I don't even have to live on Heirani Motu. I'll work remotely from Florida.

Vanessa and I had agreed we would have no groomsmen or bridesmaids, just the two of us standing at the altar. We are on a beach, but this Florida, not the South Pacific. Our five-year-old granddaughter will be the flower girl, and our three-year-old grandson will be the ring bearer. That's our whole wedding delegation, and it's exactly how we want it.

When the wedding march begins, I get a little choked up watching Vanessa's father lead her down the aisle for the second, to the same man. She has tears trickling down her cheeks as she stops beside me. Since we've been married before, we both agreed to wear normal clothes, not wedding gear. Her pale blue dress complements her blue eyes, and my suit without a tie does me just fine.

I barely notice the vows, reciting them by rote because I can't see anything but Vanessa. She is the most beautiful woman in the world, and age has done nothing to diminish that or the fire that always burns inside her. I can't believe we're doing this again, but it feels right.

"You may kiss the bride."

The second the officiant speaks those words, I throw my arms around Vanessa and kiss her like there's no tomorrow.

Cheers and clapping erupt behind us.

The second we peel our lips apart and face the crowd, our children stand up and link their hands, then start counting down. "Three, two, one—The second time's the charm!"

They throw their linked hands up and whoop.

Kids. They can be very annoying sometimes, but also unbelievably wonderful. We rush down the aisle but stop to hug our kids, grandkids, and parents. When Nicole hugs me, she whispers, "Don't make us do this a third time. Make each other happy forever, okay?"

"You got it, kiddo."

We opted for a small reception to go along with the small wedding. We prefer to think of it as intimate. While Vanessa is dancing with her father, James and Holly sit down at our table with me. After the obligatory congratulations, they share some news of their own. Vanessa has just returned and settles onto my lap.

"They have news," I tell her. "But they haven't shared it yet."

James grins. "Holly and I are taking a month-long holiday."

"Are you shutting the resort down?"

"No. We've brought in an expert to take over as general manager in my absence. Val and Eve know him well, and they're certain he can handle the job. Emilio didn't feel ready yet to handle the entire resort on his own."

Vanessa wraps her arms around my neck. "I'm glad you guys are taking some time off. You haven't been married long, and Holly confided to me that you never had a real honeymoon either."

"That's true." He slides an arm across Holly's shoulders. "It's about bloody time, isn't it, darling?"

Holly kisses his cheek. "Damn straight, honey."

I stand up with Vanessa in my arms. "I think it's time for the bride and groom to make their exit. Don't you?"

"Absolutely."

Our immediate family traipses outside with us—and yes, I'm still carrying Vanessa—and we say goodbye again. We had our honeymoon on Heirani Motu, though we weren't married then. So instead of running off to a South Pacific paradise, we're partying here at home in Florida with our family. That's the perfect way to celebrate our rekindled romance.

But we will spend one night at a swanky hotel on the beach.

In the limo, Vanessa snuggles up to me. "Thank you for deceiving me, Craig."

"You're welcome."

"We might never have found each other again if you hadn't pulled that little stunt."

"That's true." I draw her close. "But it was the magic of Heirani Motu that brought us back together."

Never in my life would I have guessed I would call an island magical and claim that it healed my broken marriage. But it's true. A nudist resort changed my life, and I will always be grateful that Vanessa took a crazy chance on a free vacation gifted to her anonymously.

Yeah, I'm one lucky guy.

Did you love

Natural Deception?

Visit
AnnaDurand.com

to subscribe to her newsletter

for updates on forthcoming books in this series

&

to receive free gifts for signing up!

Anna Durand is a bestselling, multi-award-winning author of contemporary and paranormal romance. Her books have earned bestseller status on every major retailer and wonderful reviews from readers around the world. But that's the boring spiel. Here are the really cool things you want to know about Anna!

Born on Lackland Air Force Base in Texas, Anna grew up moving here, there, and everywhere thanks to her dad's job as an instructor pilot. She's lived in Texas (twice), Mississippi, California (twice), Michigan (twice), and Alaska—and now Ohio.

As for her writing, Anna has always made up stories in her head, but she didn't write them down until her teen years. Those first awful books went into the trash can a few years later, though she learned a lot from those stories. Eventually, she would pen her first romance novel, the paranormal romance *Willpower*, and she's never looked back since.

Want even more details about Anna? Get access to her extended bio when you subscribe to her newsletter and download the free bonus ebook, *Hot Scots Confidential*. You'll also get hot deleted scenes, character interviews, fun facts, and more! Plus you'll receive the short story *Tempted by a Kiss* and mutliple bonus chapters in both ebook and audiobook formats.

Visit AnnaDurand.com to sign up.